Spindle and Dagger

To survivors
All of us

Spindle
and
Dagger

J. Anderson Coats

CANDLEWICK PRESS

Copyright © 2020 by J. Anderson Coats

First edition 2020

Library of Congress Catalog Card Number pending
ISBN 978-1-5362-0777-4

19 20 21 22 23 24 LBM 10 9 8 7 6 5 4 3 2 1

Printed in Melrose Park, IL, U.S.A.

This book was typeset in Adobe Garamond Pro.

Candlewick Press
99 Dover Street
Somerville, Massachusetts 02144

visit us at www.candlewick.com

Welsh Royal houses

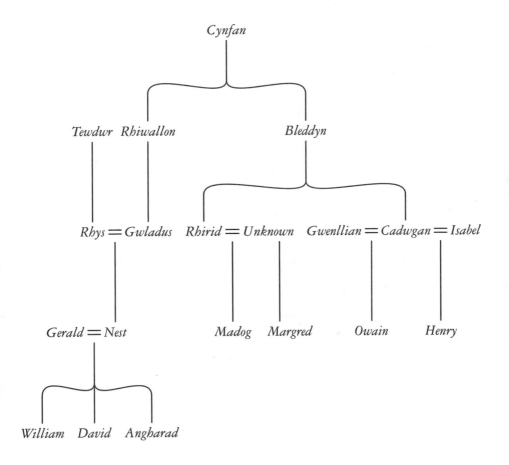

Wales
· 1109–1110 ·

(1) Aberaeron

(2) Llyssun

(3) The fort near the stream

(4) The fort Owain burns

(5) The river fort

(6) The harbor town

(7) Waterford

(8) Rathmore

(9) The Dyfed port

(10) The border fort

(11) Worthen

(12) The unlawful castle

(13) Caeriw

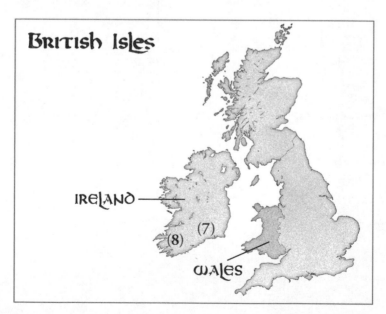

British Isles

IRELAND

(8)   (7)

WALES

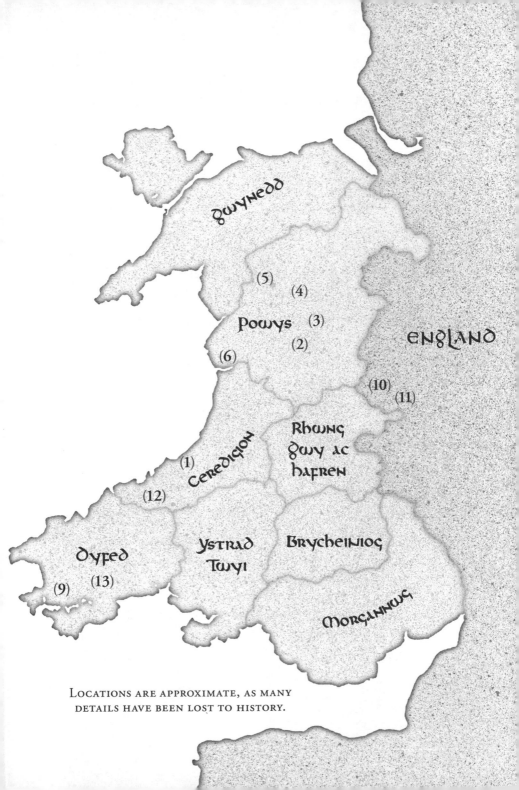

Gwynedd

England

(5)

(4)

Powys (3)

(2)

(6)

(10)

(11)

Rhwng
Gwy ac
Hafren

(1) Ceredigion

(12)

Ystrad
Tywi

Brycheiniog

Dyfed

(9) (13)

Morgannwg

LOCATIONS ARE APPROXIMATE, AS MANY
DETAILS HAVE BEEN LOST TO HISTORY.

Pronouncing Welsh Words

There is no single way to pronounce things in Welsh. The language has developed along regional lines over hundreds of years. This guide is intended to help English-speaking readers enjoy *Spindle and Dagger.*

In general, consonant sounds in Welsh are the same as those in English (for example, *d* as in *dog*). Vowels can be long or short, and *y* and *w* often function as vowels. Welsh has some letters composed of two characters together. It's important to distinguish them from the individual characters.

In terms of pronunciation, a good rule of thumb is that the stress generally falls on the second-to-last syllable. Welsh is more or less a phonetic language; you pronounce all the letters as they appear, and none are silent.

  c always a hard sound, as in *cat* (never a soft *s* sound, as in *cent*)

 dd a hard *th* sound, as in *the* (note that Welsh also has a letter *th,* which is softer, as in *thin*)

  f a *v* sound, as in *very*

 ff an *f* sound, as in *fish*

  g always a hard sound, as in *great* (never a soft *g* sound, as in *gentle*)

 ll does not have a direct English equivalent, but sounds a bit like the *tl* sound in *little*

w in words with more than one syllable, an *uh* sound, as in *pull;* in words with a single syllable, an *oo* sound, as in *loom*

y in the last syllable of a word, a short *i* sound, as in *it;* in any other syllable, a short *u* sound, as in *fun*

Welsh-speaking readers will note that I use only one form of *penteulu.* I hope I might be forgiven this small concession to an English-speaking audience.

December 1109

ORDINARY FAMILIES LOOK TO HOLY DAYS TO GATHER
and share a big meal and get rosy with ale and dance caroles and
hear the news.

I like to think I'd know ordinary if I saw it.

At last year's Christmas feast, there were three drunken fist-
fights, several black eyes, and an "accidental" lapse in courtesy
that involved a plate of turnips in sauce. We left three days early,
before Owain's father could throw us out.

Owain promised he'd behave himself this year, which I
strongly suspect means drinking his weight in claret and leading
the late-night singing of vulgar ballads. If you can call that noise
singing.

At the very least, fewer broken noses would be nice.

I'm packing my rucksack by the curtained bed in the corner
of the hall. Gowns, hose, warm woolen undergarments, and my

ball. Owain's little cousin will want a rematch after our game at Michaelmas. I also find the toy mouse I made for her from nubby scraps of linen.

Llywelyn penteulu is barking orders to speed our departure feastward, and the lads are tripping over one another to carry them out. None of them wants trouble from Owain's warband chief, especially not when he's harried. Llywelyn penteulu could be standing anywhere in the hall, but he's standing near me because it amuses him that I stutter whenever I must speak to him.

"Ah . . . you packed yet?"

One of the men of Owain's teulu, come to fetch me. I say *men.* It's the newest one—Rhys, I think—a lad who doesn't look a day over four and ten summers, the one the others still mock mercilessly for being sick all over himself during his first raid.

"Soon." The toy mouse's paws are coming unstitched where they attach to the body. Margred's at that age when well-meaning mothers and aunts start pushing rosewater behind the ears and milkwashes for the complexion, so I'm of the opinion she needs toys more than ever.

"Ah . . ." Rhys was beaten in only months ago and struggles with how to address me. The warbanders avoid me if they can and call me nothing at all, and they've likely told him to do the same. "It's just that the sun's almost up, and I've still got my own—"

"What was that, pisser?" Llywelyn penteulu rounds on Rhys,

and both of us flinch. "You afraid of girls? Because by now I sorely hope you know enough to step to it when given a task."

Rhys swallows. Chances are he's not afraid of most girls, but he might be a little afraid of me. One of the lads has doubtless told him I once stabbed a man through the neck with a fire iron, and it's no secret where I sleep at night.

"It's all right. I'm ready now." I smile an apology at Rhys as I stuff the toy into my rucksack along with my sewing kit so I can fix it later. "Come, you can —"

"You're burning daylight, lad." Owain appears behind Llywelyn penteulu's boar-solid shoulders and tilts a pointed glance at the open hall door. "It's like you *want* to be set upon by Normans."

"S-so it's true, then. There are Normans out there. Waiting." Rhys has been among the lads long enough to know that most of what they tell him is horse manure, but still he draws a shaky breath and says, "I've heard that Normans are butchers. That they're the scum of England who've come to the kingdoms of Wales because they take joy in killing, and here they can be as brutal as they want."

"Hell yes, it's true," Owain replies, bluff and cheerful, "but there's no shame standing in dread of terrible things. Or terrible men."

Rhys hesitates. "But *you're* not afraid."

"No reason to be." Owain shrugs with a simple, carefree confidence that never fails to send a chill down my back. "Saint Elen protects me."

"Owain ap Cadwgan can't be killed, not by blade nor blow nor poison." I say it calm and sure, the way I imagine Saint Elen would if she were here, because these lads cannot hear it enough times.

"And here's what I must do for that protection." Owain grins and pulls me against him with one hand sprawled over my backside. "Here she is, my Elen, good and close. Who am I to ignore the will of a saint?"

Rhys glances at me again through long, tangly curls. He is deliberately keeping his eyes off Owain's hand on my haunch. There are no secrets in a warband. Rhys is not asking because any of this is new to him. He's been told that Saint Elen keeps Owain safe in and out of the field, and he certainly believes a saint is capable of such things. He's just not sure why. It's not every day that Almighty God sees fit to lay a special blessing on the likes of Owain ap Cadwgan through the intercession of one of His saints.

"So you'll see her packed and ready, then? Good." Owain claps Rhys on the shoulder and turns to leave.

"This little pisser thinks he's above the task," Llywelyn penteulu says. "He has better things to do. He thinks that little of your safety."

Owain stops midstride. "Beg pardon. What was that?"

I fight down the urge to speak for Rhys. It's hard to begrudge him uncertainty, but it's too dangerous for him to keep it.

Rhys shuffles. "My lord . . . it's not . . ."

"Not what?" Owain leans close to Rhys, eyes in slits. "You think this is rubbish? You don't believe a saint protects me?"

Llywelyn penteulu steps to Owain's shoulder, and together they're a shield wall as they glower down at Rhys. I edge backward, slow, slow, till I'm clear.

"Draw your blade, then," Owain says to Rhys in a low, dangerous voice, "and let's see if it's true."

"My lord, I never said — no, of course it's true." Rhys tries to square up. "It's just that Einion ap Tewdwr told me so, and anything he says is usually worth its weight in shit."

I can't help but smirk. At least Rhys has learned that lesson well.

"All those bastard Normans out there, every last one would give his right nut to cut me to pieces, and none of them can. Saint Elen will not let that happen. No man in all the kingdoms of Wales can say the same." Owain drops his fighting stance and bares his teeth into a smile. "Likely no little pisser, either, for that matter."

Llywelyn penteulu pulls Rhys close with a fistful of cloak. "Are we clear, boy?"

Rhys nods without looking up. His breath comes unsteady. *Teulu* means both *warband* and *family*. A warband is like a family. More than a family. Brothers in arms over brothers in blood.

"Good. Then look to Elen." Owain adjusts his sword-belt. "We'd best be off soon. It won't do to be late to the feast. Not when my stepmother will supposedly grace us with her presence."

He says it mocking, but I stop where I stand. Owain has told me exactly three things about his stepmother: she's the daughter of a Norman knight, she'd tempt a saint to sin, and she's younger than he is. Isabel de Say has been two years wed to Owain's father, and finding her place in her new husband's kingdom can't have been easy. Strange tongue, strange customs, sharing a bed with someone who's spent his entire adult life and a good portion of his youth killing Normans like her who were trying to seize his lands. If there was ever another girl in search of ordinary, it has to be her.

Isabel and I have never been properly introduced, not even at their wedding, but she's sure to look at me and see herself. A girl out of place and in need of allies and sympathy.

Owain's kin look through me and past me, but Isabel's someone who might meet my eye across the room and nod, like she sees me and doesn't care who knows. Someone who might be able to carve me out a place in this turbulent family and leave me to occupy it in peace. I won't come with empty hands, either. There must be things she still struggles with. Words she can't say right. Or mayhap no one has invited her to play at ball.

At this year's Christmas feast, I may not dance caroles or get rosy with ale, but I will steer Owain away from trouble and find a way to make his stepmother a friend, for Owain ap Cadwgan is the closest thing I have to a family.

Not by blood. Not by marriage.

Because of Saint Elen.

†

THE LADS TRAVEL PRECISE AND DELIBERATE IN TWO
columns of nine with a spear-length between men, Owain heading one column and Llywelyn penteulu the other. I follow at
the end at elbows with Rhys. Every now and then he'll smile
sidelong to prove he's not bothered minding me.

There's a soft snick of brush, and in the next heartbeat men
are on us with short swords, a dozen men who rush like ghosts
through the still, snow-lined trees. The lads draw steel and
fall hard on the attackers. There's a burst of shouting in harsh
French, the solid sound of bodies colliding, the clatterclunk of
metal on metal. The hiss of a name—Gerald of Windsor.

Normans. Butchers invading the kingdoms of Wales, but not
just for killing. They've come to take what they can, and they'd
have the kingdom of Powys from Owain's father. His province
of Ceredigion as well.

Owain is amid it. If he dies, no saint can help me. If he dies, I'm done for.

The fight is sharp and grim and over quickly. Three Normans lie slain, and the rest are pelting through the greenwood toward wherever they came from. The lads stand panting, their eyes wild and their sword-arms fidgety. Owain is whole and unharmed, and I thank every saint who ever lived even as I struggle to keep my breakfast down.

"Oh, Christ. Dear God Almighty, no."

Owain's voice is raw and desperate, both hands shoved through his hair. The man crumpled at his feet isn't Norman. It's Llywelyn penteulu, and Owain is pushing away the lads who have gathered and dropping to his knees at the side of his warband chief and oldest friend.

"Die," I whisper, and the greenwood falls away and I'm up against the steading wall held fast, cold everywhere *can't struggle,* and Miv is wailing but there are other cries too, panicked, angry, and faint amid that noise is a haphazard shuddery weeping that turns my stomach.

Oh saints, no. Not the echoes again. They'd all but faded to shadows.

"We've got to do something." Owain's wild gaze rakes the lads, all standing like pallbearers, red-eyed, shuffling, looking to the branches above and the torn-up mud and everywhere and nowhere.

"What of her?" Einion ap Tewdwr steps forward, hopeful and urgent. "The miracle girl?"

I freeze. I would have to touch him. Skin to skin. The blood. The *smell* of him.

But every last one of the lads is looking to me. Owain, too, even as his color drains and cold mud climbs the hem of his tunic.

I've never once used the word *miracle,* though if I'm honest, I have let it hang there.

So I make myself go, but when I get to Llywelyn penteulu's side, it's plain there's no doing for him. Not by me. Not by anyone. The Norman blade caught him across the neck and took a wedge of wet red flesh with it. His stare is already going blank.

I should beg Saint Elen to intercede with the Almighty the way she did for Owain, but I don't. Instead I look Owain in the eye and say as steady as I can, "Saint Elen kept you safe. Did you see how she knocked that blade aside? Every man of those Normans wanted you dead. Are you dead?"

Einion's mouth falls open and he chokes on a few broken curses. Owain stifles a shuddering breath that's suspiciously like a sob. Then he presses his forehead against Llywelyn penteulu's and grips his friend's hand and chokes out some odd garble of the paternoster and last rites.

In less time than it takes to piss, Llywelyn penteulu is dead.

At my elbow, Owain sits back on his heels, panting sharp and shallow. He scrubs a wrist over wet cheeks as he regards the body. Then he reaches out a shaking hand and closes his warband chief's dull staring eyes. At length he whispers, "Saint Elen kept me."

"Yes, she did," I reply to my knees as they gouge the bloody, mud-slick ground, "because she looks to you always."

We stay pressed together for a long moment. Then all at once, Owain rocks to his feet and stomps a handful of paces away. He tips his head to the sky and roars, "Gerald of Windsor! You miserable Norman bastard! You're a dead man! You hear me? *I will find you and kill you!*"

I scrape blood from my hands with my handkerchief. He's dead. Llywelyn penteulu is actually dead. I will never again catch his eye by mischance. I will never again shiver outside a door waiting on his departure. Every echo of him will soon be gone.

The lads drift toward Owain, gathering, murmuring *Saint Elen* and *hairsbreadth* and *blessed.* They stand together like a flock of crows, shoulder to shoulder, solid as a fist. Now and then one of them glances at me, crossing himself, slow and reverent like he just walked out of mass.

"We mustn't linger here." Einion ap Tewdwr seizes Owain's sleeve. "Gerald and his bastard Normans know where we are now."

Owain nods without looking at him. He's still trembling. Einion pulls several of the lads aside. They dig through their rucksacks and one produces a length of canvas. Owain crouches alone beneath a nearby oak while the lads wrap the body. He looks young of a sudden. Not like a man with almost twenty summers who's been in the field since four and ten. Not like a king's son who's been training with arms since he could hold a sword, always with an eye to borders that would one day be his to defend.

I should go to Owain, kneel beside him, offer something comforting. Not moments ago, there was a death in his family. His most trusted advisor. His brother in everything but blood.

I don't trust my knees to work properly, though.

It's one thing to know how Owain and his warband spend their days. Another thing entirely to see how easily something as simple as a journey can go wrong. Another thing besides to swear to him up and down that he has a saint's protection when every word of it is a lie.

He can die by blade. He can die in a drunken brawl or a fall from his horse or by choking on a chicken bone. He nearly died today, right in front of me, because Saint Elen has made no promises to Owain ap Cadwgan.

None of what I tell him is true.

Three summers ago, I spun this playact out of some choice falsehoods on the thin hope that Owain might believe it worth his while to safeguard me if I had something he wanted. I should not be surprised he took to the idea like a bull to rutting. Not when he's convinced he can do what he likes, say what he likes, rough up who he likes, take any chances he likes — all because a saint stands over his shoulder and keeps him from harm. Whether he deserves harm or not.

Mayhap Saint Elen is keeping Owain safe in spite of me, or possibly just to spite me. Or it might be that she's merely watching, amused, to see how my playact turns out. God Almighty sent the saints to listen to us and help us, but why they do anything is a mystery. I can't command Saint Elen or persuade her, but I can talk to her.

So I do. Head down, knees muddy, throat choked. I pray silently to Saint Elen of the Hosts who built roads throughout the kingdoms of Wales long ago to help armies march to war. The saint whose name I share, who's listened to me patiently since I was so small that I asked for sweets and ribbons. This prayer is one she knows chapter and verse.

> *Thank you for everything you've done for me.*
> *Thank you for understanding.*
> *If you did save Owain's life today, thank you most*
> *especially for that.*

This can't be the first time Owain's nearly met his end out here. He's not wrong when he says that every Norman in Wales would dearly love to cut him to pieces. And more than one Welshman would hold him down. Women, too. The life of someone like Owain ap Cadwgan is a flimsy thing to hang a playact on, but in three years, he has only cuts and bruises to show from hundreds of raids and skirmishes and fights and brawls.

This is the first time I've seen it, though. The first time I've watched Normans go after him, brutal and single-minded. The first time in a very long while that I thought my playact might fall apart and I'd die at the hands of Owain's grieving, deceived, and furious warband.

So there must be something to it. Even the smallest word from a saint would be enough to keep Owain safe should the Almighty will it so. At the very least I know Saint Elen is watching. I can't see her, but there can be no other reason I can climb to my feet right now. No other reason I can move to where Owain is standing alone and take his trembling, blood-smeared hand.

THE SKY IS ALL BUT DARK WHEN WE REACH THE FORT
of Aberaeron. I'm wrung out from tensing at every brush-twitch
and trying to seem sorrowful for a man I'd see fed to pigs, but
time has come, so I call up my miracle face — wise, unruffled,
everlasting confident. The lads have leather armor, and I have
Saint Elen.

Someone must have run ahead to alert Owain's father we'd
arrived, for Cadwgan ap Bleddyn is standing in the hall doorway
in a finely cut Norman-looking tunic and shiny leather boots.

He's by himself. Mayhap Owain was wrong about his stepmother finally coming to a family gathering.

No. Isabel must merely be busy elsewhere. Holding a Christmas feast is no small task, not when you're wed to a king, and
this family will make it no easier with their swagger and boast-
ing and eye-blackening. I can offer to help, and then we'll share

a honey cake and she'll invite me to spin with the wives, and before long I'll always sit with them, even if Isabel isn't there to beckon me over.

Cadwgan gestures to the hall door, and Owain heads inside. When I follow, Cadwgan cuts in front of me so I must trail them both like a wolfhound. In the shaft of doorway light, he extends his wrist to Owain before collaring him into a fierce, brief hug. "Christ Jesus, lad. I just heard. Men don't come better than Llywelyn ap Ifor."

"He's been with me since the beginning. When I wasn't any older than that little pisser." Owain nods at Rhys helping to carry the body toward the chapel. "I swear I *felt* Saint Elen knocking that Norman blade away from me. But it . . . it struck Llywelyn instead."

Cadwgan draws a long, patient breath. "Son, it's Christmas. You've just had a gut-wrench loss. Can we leave it there? I've no wish to argue. Especially about something we will never see eye to eye on."

Something is definitely not the worst thing Cadwgan has ever called me. In fact, it's a promising sign that he's trying to avoid a fight about Saint Elen instead of needling Owain into one.

"It was Gerald of Windsor, wasn't it?" Cadwgan asks quietly.

Owain glares at nothing and murmurs, "He's a dead man."

"That Norman whoreson will kill either one of us on sight, given half a chance. He wants my kingdom in the worst way, and he won't get it by other means." Cadwgan shifts uncomfortably. "I . . . feared the worst when my runner said there was a body."

"I will not fall, Da." Owain holds out an arm dappled with Llywelyn penteulu's blood. "It will not happen."

"I've no doubt you believe that," Cadwgan mutters. "She's made it very easy for you."

Owain makes a show of clutching his chest, staggering into me, and gasping, "Ooh! Da! That kind of cruelty is what'll be the end of me!"

Cadwgan groans and shoves Owain, but not in an angry way. Owain pushes his father back, and the two of them stand together for a long moment, likely thinking of their slain friend.

I'm thinking how it's not like Cadwgan can be rid of me, and how much easier it would be for everyone if he'd simply show a thimbleful of courtesy on occasions like this. He doesn't even have to mean it. I'm thinking how it will be when Isabel looks forward to seeing me at gatherings like this. When it's not just Cadwgan's oldest son who enjoys my company, but his wife as well. Two people even a king must heed.

†

CADWGAN CALLS A SERVANT TO SHOW OWAIN WHERE
he can clean up before the feast. He follows wearily, shrugging
off his bloodstained tunic as he goes, and Cadwgan waits, arms
folded, till I back out of the hall and into the freezing yard.

Across the way is the maidens' quarters, but Cadwgan is
still watching from the door, and I don't want to bring trouble
on the girl cousins. So I wander the yard until I find a blind
alley behind the laundry where women wring out and hang
undergarments. It's private enough, especially as the yard fills
up with guests for the feast, and sheltered from the wind, so I
borrow a bucket and rag from a harried laundress, strip down,
and scrub fast.

My breath comes out in puffs, and I curse December as I
slosh the rag through the steaming water. I wash my arms and
feet ten thousand times to scour what's left of Llywelyn penteulu

off me and be done with him forever. The water turns murky. Colder with every pass. I grind the rag harder down my legs. Across my belly. My skin starts to hurt, and it's a long moment before I realize I'm scrubbing where I'm already clean, as if I can scour clear to the bone.

I can't. I've already tried.

I'm as clean as I'm going to get and halfway to frostbite besides, so I struggle into my new gown, the red one Owain brought me just for Christmas. I adjust the cuffs and notice the dried smear of blood.

I wonder what she looked like, where she lived. I wonder how Owain came upon her and in what state he left her. Mayhap she gave the gown up willingly, just trembled a hand toward a coffer or garment rod while she cowered in a corner. Or perhaps she stood her ground and clenched her fists.

Picked up a fire iron.

I plunge the cuff into new water and scrub. I scrub so hard that fibers come loose and my fingernails ache. Then it's clean. No traces of what came before this moment. No echoes.

After I'm dressed, I'm not ready to face the hall. Not yet. The windows are bright in the maidens' quarters and Margred answers my knock, bouncing on her toes and swinging embroidery that's trailing threads. She's grown at least a handswidth, and she's rounder through the hips, even though she's still wearing a child's straight-waist shift dress. Her face lights up, and she squeals and pulls me inside, even as her nurse sternly reminds her that she shouldn't just throw open the door to any strange knocking. That nurse is not wrong, but Margred is already hugging me and rattling on about how much she missed me and did I bring my ball and mayhap there'll be honey cake at supper, and oh saints, her carefree chatter is like a warm drink of cider. I hold up the toy mouse and she snatches it playfully, holds it to her face, and spins like a child half her age.

"You want to see my new gown?" Margred kneels by a coffer and perches the mouse on her head while she swings open the lid. "Papa says perhaps next Christmas I can sit with him and Mama in the hall!"

I meet the nurse's eyes over Margred's head. Dresses are the last thing I want to talk about. Next year sometime, when she has twelve summers, Margred will start eating in the hall so the nobility can see what her father has on offer, and that's when I will start to lose her.

I let her show me, though. The gown is blue and grown-up. She and her mother put in every stitch.

My cuff is still damp. Clammy against my wrist. I bump Margred's shoulder cheerfully and say, "I did bring my ball. Want to play tomorrow after mass? We'll tread goal lines in the snow in the courtyard."

Margred grins and tells me all the girl cousins are spoiling for a match. She closes the coffer lid, the gown forgotten, and dances her toy mouse on her knees. We talk of her horse and the garden she's planning for spring until serving boys turn up with trays of food. It's cozy here, and quiet, but Isabel would never come to the maidens' quarters, so I wish Margred and her nurse a good meal and head across the courtyard toward the hall's glowing door.

Inside, noblemen are crowded at long tables, laughing and drinking mead and talking over one another while Aberaeron's priest looks on like a proud grandfather. There are women, too, wives and sisters and mothers, glittering in finery, gathered in tight, impenetrable knots. Owain is sitting at the high table, dressed in a gray tunic and holding out a mug to a cupbearer. I move to join him, dodging hips and elbows, but I'm not five steps inside when Cadwgan blocks my way.

"Kitchen's across the yard by the wall," he says. "They'll give you a tray. I imagine the sleeping chamber will be more to your liking."

I know better than to take the bait. "Owain would have me near him. It's Christmas."

"Which is why you will not sit at my son's right hand in my hall." Cadwgan doesn't add *like a wife,* but he might as well.

I square up and say, "I saved his life."

"After you stabbed him!"

No. That was Rhael. She picked up the butcher knife and pressed the fire iron into my hands, and we pushed Miv's cradle into the darkest corner of the steading and stood shoulder to shoulder while the clatter in the dooryard grew ever louder.

I try to dodge around Cadwgan, but he seizes my arm and roughly turns me so I'm facing the hall door and the cold night—only we come face-to-face with Isabel. She's wearing a green silk gown that must have cost a small fortune, and her veil is crisp and tidy and perfect. Her cheeks are pink, like Margred's.

This isn't how I planned our meeting. I pictured somewhere quiet. Private. Somewhere I could be of help. I'm not good in a crowd. But now's my chance, and I've been practicing since I learned I'd have this moment.

A greeting, friendly but not too familiar.

A gracious thanks for her hospitality.

A witty, lighthearted observation about the lunacy of this family that'll make her grin and take my hands and say something like *I feel the exact same way.*

Isabel glances at Cadwgan, then me, then at his hand still gripping my elbow hard enough to sting. Then me again, without looking away. Her face is blank like a pond on a still morning.

This is the first time I'm standing before Owain's stepmother, and I'm trading harsh words with her husband, who's holding me suspiciously close, and I cannot muster the sense God gave a goat to explain myself.

My throat chokes up. I can't even babble. But then Isabel silently peels Cadwgan's hand off my arm and leads him toward some guests by the hearth. Neither of them looks back.

Cadwgan was ready to throw me out of the hall. All she had to do was move aside and let him, but instead she stepped in. She did it with grace and tact, in a way no one else could, so Cadwgan could save face and I could walk away.

Isabel just helped me.

By the time this feast is over, she and I could be chatting every day, sharing a hearth bench and giggling over wine. By summer, we could be friends. By this time next year, the idea that anyone in Owain's family might think to show me the smallest discourtesy might be a distant, unpleasant memory.

I KEEP SNEAKING GLANCES AT ISABEL NEAR THE hearth, hoping she's sneaking glances at me. If she is, I can't tell, since Cadwgan's back is blocking my view. The feast will last till Epiphany, and that's se'ennights from now. Plenty of time to invent a reason to pass the hours together, and I'll be damn sure it won't be when I need something from her.

For now, what I need is somewhere to stand so I don't look like a child banished to the naughty corner. Cadwgan expressly forbade me to sit with Owain at the high table, and I'd just as soon avoid his temper. Margred's still safely in the maidens' quarters. If Isabel was anywhere but next to Cadwgan, I could—

Owain catches my eye with a smile I know very well, then makes a showy gesture to the empty place at his elbow. So he's decided to start stirring the pot early this year and make his father the first target.

Well. I can still hope for fewer black eyes, I reckon.

When I reach Owain's side, there's nowhere for me to sit. The place at his right is clearly Cadwgan's even though it's empty, and Owain's cousin Madog has taken the spot at his left. I try hard to think well of Madog because he's Margred's brother, but tonight he makes that extra difficult as he glances me up and down, fold and drape, slow and deep and hungry.

"You some kind of warbander, honey? You gonna cut me?" Madog's mug is half full, but it can't be his first, for he's *thisclose* to being out of turn.

Owain catches my hand, kisses my palm, then lifts his brows at his cousin. "When was the last time you looked twice at a woman in the shadows, whether she hid a blade in her skirts? Shove down."

Madog grumbles but moves enough to make a place for me at Owain's left. I sit, then reach for an oatcake and break it into crumbs that I line up in neat rows. Everyone watched Owain beckon to me. The nobles, their wives, every servant down to the cupbearers. They watched Owain bid Madog move. They're all watching me and muttering behind their hands and speculating.

Owain loves it when they speculate. He says the more they're guessing about me, the less they're watching what he's doing.

"You ought to take me on as penteulu when we ravage south into Dyfed." Madog reaches across me to poke Owain's shoulder with the butt end of his meat knife. "I've never been in a warband that had its own whore."

I keep crumbling. As speculations go, that one is definitely not new, and anyone who spends even trifling moments near Owain's warband does well to realize how untrue it is.

But Owain sets down his mug and turns, slow and deliberate, to face his cousin. In a brittle-calm voice he says, "Tell me that you did not just have the stones to suggest in the public of my father's hall that you of all men should even be *considered* to replace the likes of Llywelyn ap Ifor as the chief of my warband."

"Come now, Owain, no disrespect intended, but it's plain obvious you need a penteulu, and I'm the best choice."

"He was a brother to me," Owain says in small, sharp words, "and his body is barely cold and bleeding all over the floor of my father's chapel and we are at a *Christmas feast* and I am a guest here or so help me God I would make your mother weep to look upon you."

Madog scowls. "Christ. Just trying to lift your spirits. I thought it would ease your mind to have a good penteulu when we sack Dyfed."

"I have not yet decided who will follow my friend as penteulu. I'm eating my meat and enjoying the company — some of it, anyway. There'll be time enough for such things later."

If Madog is at Owain's right hand, organizing drills in the yard of whatever fort we're staying in and imposing marching orders and offering counsel and sorting out disputes, I'll see so much more of Margred. Not just on holy days and at weddings and burials, but at informal gatherings, too. We'll be all but kin. I'll be the voice in her ear as she's eating with the grown-ups in the hall, handing her toys instead of rosewater and keeping her running up and down a ball court for as long as I can, and one day years and years from now, she'll be one of the wives who'll let me stay and sit and spin and simply *be*.

Madog is not my favorite of Owain's kin, but he's right about one thing. He is the best choice for penteulu. None of Owain's brothers by blood are old enough, and no other male relations are ready or trustworthy. He's got to be wrong about the other, though. They can't be raiding Dyfed. That province is armed to the teeth and bristling with castles and crawling with Normans who've come from England for no other reason than to take land from men like Cadwgan ap Bleddyn. Even a ruthless warband would soon be run to ground.

"You'd best not take too much time." Madog's face is scarlet, and he hunches over his mug of mead. Owain doesn't hear him, though. Cadwgan has taken his seat, and the two of them are discussing something in growls. Me sitting here, like as not, and I brace for the argument that will doubtless get mean in a hurry.

But I hear only names of people who aren't me and places to be won or lost. It's nothing I haven't heard a thousand times, but with different names and different places. Cadwgan's enemies and allies turn their cloaks one way or another depending on the day or the se'ennight or the month, depending on who ambushes whose fort and who castrates who, and he does the same to them. Someone may be an enemy now, but by Easter he may be attacking someone else on Cadwgan's behalf. Or the other way around. Or Cadwgan may set them both on a third enemy he hasn't even made yet.

I've never been happier to be overlooked. It'll give me a chance to approach Isabel once more, since she's taken her seat on Cadwgan's other side. She's chattering cheerfully to the woman next to her, pointing to her guest's necklet and running an admiring hand down her gown sleeve. When Isabel pauses to take a sip of wine, I catch her eye and smile. I'm trying to thank her for what she did earlier, and with Owain and Cadwgan between us discussing raids, it's the perfect chance to point out something we share. *You know men—ignoring us to speak of bloodshed.*

But Isabel does not return my smile. She lifts one brow and deliberately turns back to her guest, cups her hand over the woman's ear, and begins to whisper. The nasty sow grins and darts her eyes to me before snickering like I just stepped in something.

Oh saints. I've misjudged all this. Badly.

Isabel is not an outsider. She never has been. She's the wife of the king of Powys. She's well on her way to charming this disreputable lot into good behavior. She's wearing a gown that never had blood on the cuffs.

She is nothing like me.

I can't do this myself. I can't just decide there's a place for me here and stand in it. If I could, I'd have done it by now. If I don't have someone like Isabel on my side, I will always stand apart.

†

THE MEAL GOES WELL PAST SUNDOWN. VENISON AND
savories and mug after mug of wine and mead. I don't so much
as look Isabel's way again. She was not helping me. She was
removing her husband from my presence. I didn't see it. I should
have seen it.

Down the table, there's a burst of cackling muffled by hands.

This is the nest of vipers Margred will put her foot into next
year. Sweet, kindhearted Margred, who has promised we'll be
friends forever, come what may. She's still young enough to make
those kinds of promises. She's that sure of her place in this difficult family and that innocent of what her promise might cost.

It's full winter dark when I follow Owain across the
snow-skiffed yard to the sleeping chamber. He leads me near
the banked fire and pulls his blanket over us both, and we lie

together in the dying emberlight. Afterward, he holds me close and I rest my head against his shoulder. His arm across my back is comforting and solid, and his sun-browned hand over my hip looks like armor.

I open my mouth to ask Owain how long we'll be stuck here and if there'll be gingerbread and whether he minds if I spend the morrow with Margred and the cousins, but before I can, he wraps his other arm around me and into my hair he murmurs, "I can't believe he's gone."

I can't say how much I glory in Llywelyn penteulu soon to be food for worms six feet beneath God's green earth. I dare not speak ill of a single one of Owain's brothers, living or dead.

The patter rises to save me, smooth and well-trodden like a path I've walked a thousand times. "Saint Elen kept you from harm, just as she always does."

"Not an armslength from me," he whispers. "I turned . . . and the blade was already falling, and I . . . shouted, but . . ."

Owain slides a finger along the scar beneath his arm. It's a slim, wine-colored line of flesh that runs about the length of my finger. It looks like nothing. Mayhap a ridge worn into his skin from too-tight leather armor or a scratch by a stray fingernail during bedsport.

He almost bled out from that wound, though. Owain ap Cadwgan would have died that day, were it not for me.

"Saint Elen looks to you always," I repeat.

He lets out a long, trembling breath and tightens his arms around me, but I don't snuggle against him this time because now I'm looking at that scar and thinking how in two motions I could kill Owain ap Cadwgan.

One motion to seize the knife.

The other to cut his throat.

The dagger is within easy reach beneath a pile of clothing. I could kill him and he'd be dead. I close my eyes against a clatter in the yard. The fire iron cold in my hand as he kicked in the door. Miv crying. Blood everywhere. I begged Saint Elen for my life that day, and she gave it to me.

"When are we leaving?" I finally ask.

Owain sighs deep. "Epiphany. Would it was sooner. I'll not be good company for man or beast. My father may send us out early just to be rid of us."

Rid of *me*, he must mean. "Where are we going? The hunting lodge at Llyssun?"

"You are."

"Where are you—oh."

He and the lads will disappear into the hills and later sweep down with fire and sword on dwellings and goods belonging to some enemy of Cadwgan. They'll kill anyone who fights back and burn everything that stands and smash anything that won't burn and plunder everything of value and drive off whatever lows or grunts or bleats. They will wreck and pillage again and again until the tenants of Cadwgan's enemy have nothing but postholes and cinders and corpses, so it's known to every man that their lord is helpless to defend them.

Raids are done with steel and terror, quick like the snap of a neck. In the best of them, no one sees you coming and everyone returns alive and weighed down with plunder. In the worst, you carry a friend home wrapped in canvas and pray for his soul and drink his memory till you can barely stand.

My little playact clings to those odds.

"The northern provinces again?" I keep my eyes off that scar.

"Dyfed."

I push myself up on one elbow. "What? No. You—*what?*"

"The English king wants to conquer all the kingdoms of Wales. He can't simply invade, though." Owain smiles faintly. "The last time a king of theirs tried, he tripped over himself limping home with his nose well-bloodied."

Cadwgan's knuckles were first among those that did the bloodying. I wait for Owain to say as much, to tell the stories he must have grown up on, but instead he growls, "The English king refuses to risk himself, so he sends lackeys like Gerald of Windsor to take and hold what they can, and now Gerald governs Dyfed. Which means that patch of dirt on our southern border is a sword leveled at my father's throat. Mine, too. Which means Gerald of Windsor needs himself a humbling. So I'll give him one."

Owain is playing with a strand of my hair and completely underestimating Normans with their walls to withdraw behind and trained fighting men in coats of mail and big two-handed broadswords that can cut someone in half. Who killed Llywelyn penteulu even with armed brothers around him like two dozen sharp palisades.

"Once the lads and I burn every handswidth and carry away the plunder, I'll hunt down Gerald of bloody Windsor like the dog he is, and with my own hand cut him into small pieces and piss on every last one of them."

I peer into Owain's face, waiting for that smirk or eyebrow that'll let me in on the jest. He's staring straight ahead, eyes narrow. He's nowhere near here.

"But not before I string him up in his own dooryard," Owain goes on, "and while he hangs there writhing, I will carve the name of Llywelyn ap Ifor who he butchered without regard ten thousand times into his flesh, till his hide falls off in ribbons."

I like to think Saint Elen understands why I told Owain she'll protect him, that she pitied me for being in a place where that playact was necessary, that she tolerates it still for compassion's sake. But there is a world of difference between protection and counsel. One is standing by while Saint Elen does as she sees fit, and the other is deciding for her what she should do and say. If I dare to put words in her mouth, to make myself the saint, she will turn her back on me for sure.

So I can't tell Owain that Saint Elen said not to kill the English king's right hand in Dyfed in cold blood because no man can ignore such an act. Instead I say, carefully, "Won't the English king see that sort of killing as a personal insult? Gerald owes him everything he has. Seeking the downfall of someone so loyal does not seem wise."

"I don't seek the downfall of Gerald of bloody Windsor." Owain's voice is eerily calm, and I edge away from him bit by bit, pulling the blankets with me because I'm shivering now, and not just from the cold. "Bad enough he's lurking to the south with his eyes on my birthright. Now that he's raided my very dooryard? Now that he's killed my friend and warband chief, slaughtered him *right in front of me*? Oh, I will not merely kill Gerald of bloody Windsor now. I will preside over his complete humiliation and destruction first."

I can't tell him Saint Elen said to raid quick and fierce and leave vengeance to the Almighty, no matter how much I want to.

Owain blinks hard and scrubs a wrist over his eyes. There's a very real chance he'll sober up on the morrow and this whole thing with Gerald of Windsor will be a dull ache in the back of his throat. A ghost of something noble yet foolish and therefore forgettable. He'll name another penteulu—please let it be Madog—and he'll raid Dyfed properly, fire and sword and plunder, just like the last raid and the raid before that one.

"Betimes I think my father is jealous." Owain slides closer to me, snakes a hand around my waist, nuzzles my neck. "My stepmother may turn heads, but all he got for his pains is a patch of Norman border dirt and a worthless alliance and a nagging voice in his ear. I've a saint at my back, and all I must do to please her is keep her namesake safe from all harm and near me always."

It rolls off his tongue so easily. You'd never know that Saint Elen and her promises were straws I grasped at while I was still changing the dressings on the wound beneath his arm, when the fever that nearly put him before his Maker still muddied his thoughts enough for him to take it as gospel. He should have died that day at my sister's hands on the floor of our steading in a pool of his own blood.

I nod, though, because he's done what I told him Saint Elen required. I'm safe from all harm and near him always. I was just not careful what I asked for. Because I got it.

THE CHAPEL IS A STONE'S THROW FROM THE HALL.
It's empty this time of day, no priests around. There's no proper
door so it's cold within, a skiff of crunchy snow pushed along the
threshold. Before the altar lies the body, shrouded in linen and
dim. I mean to go further, to look upon Llywelyn penteulu well
dead, but even now I cannot.

Even this close, my throat turns to sand. My mouth goes
sour. And I am up against the steading wall and Miv is crying
and there's a body at my feet fire iron through the neck and
Llywelyn penteulu is roaring in my face. Hard to the floor cold
everywhere *can't struggle.*

Torn to pieces. Skin to skin. The *smell.*

There were others after him, but he was the first. Until they
let me up.

There's a scuffle at the chapel doorway, and Einion ap Tewdwr appears, holding a pale, swaying Rhys by one arm.

We killed them both and seized all the beasts. Einion said it like he'd killed them himself. Mayhap he had. My father would have struggled. My mother, too, but they'd have been no match for a warband.

"Miracle girl." Einion points with his knuckle. "Out here. Now."

The lads know better than to speak roughly to me. Mostly they don't speak to me at all unless it's to ask something trivial, like will I mend a tear in a tunic or refill a mug of mead. I'm too wrung out to challenge Einion on it, though, and Owain is definitely not in a humor to dress down one of his own in his father's hall while Llywelyn penteulu's body is barely cold, so I step into the bright outdoors, blinking against it.

"Stand here," Einion growls, and I'm not sure whether he's talking to me or Rhys. Einion releases Rhys and storms into the chapel. In moments he's back, and he says, "Whatever you did, there's no sign of it."

"No sign of what?"

"Marks. On the body."

I gape at him, and he scoffs. "Oh, come now. I don't for a moment believe you were paying your respects. What other reason could you have for being in there?"

I have no answer that will make sense to the likes of Einion ap Tewdwr, so instead I show him my empty hands. "I've no weapon."

"Doubtless Llywelyn penteulu's brother thought that, too. Just before you broke his neck with a fire iron to the windpipe."

Rhael told me not to be afraid. We would give them the food we'd prepared. We'd give them the animals in the byre. We would give them whatever they wanted, then they would leave. She said it clear and confident, gripping and regripping the big knife, and I believed her.

I face Einion steady on and ask, "What do you want?"

"Show her." Einion jostles Rhys forward with a shake of tunic.

Rhys merely sways like a drunk. Einion sighs and pushes up the boy's sleeve for him, revealing a deep gash the color of rancid meat. When Einion swivels Rhys's arm, the boy sucks in a breath and a flash of bone turns like a fish's silvery belly.

"Is this from the raid?" I ask. "The raid from *days* ago?"

When Einion nods, I groan, but I can hardly blame Rhys for not wanting to be called *baby* and told to grow a pair. Especially considering that worse befell one of their family that morning.

"Why did you not bring him to the court physician?"

"The boy needs a miracle as well as medicine." Einion peers at me. "What does Saint Elen say?"

I did not think. I only acted. I never used the word *miracle*.

They do, though. All the lads. All but the newest saw with their own eyes what I did for Owain, how he went from bleeding out on my steading floor to burning down forts and halls instead of lying in the cold earth. There's not a man in this warband who does not believe Owain ap Cadwgan has the protection of a saint.

"Let's have a look." I turn away from the chapel. "Help me bring him to the kitchen."

The building is all the way across the yard, and we move at Rhys's shambling pace. He holds his injured arm with the wound turned outward, and I can study it sidelong. It's bad, but nowhere near as bad as the one that almost killed Owain. I'll put the irons to it, Rhys will recover and see a miracle, God willing, and every time he's near me he'll touch that scar.

The lads of Owain's warband will see him do it, too.

The kitchen is hot and damp and thick with smells. I poke through the scatter of cutlery and implements on the trestle board, then pick a long, thin spreader and lay its rounded end in the fire. I sit on my haunches watching it heat up. There's a quiet creak of leather, and Einion kneels at my elbow. He's built like a bull, all compact muscles and a whipcrack temper. I make myself stay still. He will not touch me.

"Owain's taking it hard." Einion rubs a hand over his jaw. "He will not stop speaking of it."

He'll be seeing the blade falling. Helpless to stop it. The blood. The gasping.

"But Saint Elen did not save Llywelyn penteulu," Einion says in an oh-so-quiet voice.

"Saint Elen protects Owain." The patter rises to save me, and I let it. "She looks to him always. The rest of us are on our own."

"Seems a strange way to protect a man, removing his right hand."

I cut my eyes to Einion, but he's merely studying the fire, balanced toe and knee, ambush-still.

"Then again," he goes on, "I'm a simple fighting man. What do I know of saints and their doings? They are not motivated by our petty concerns. Like spite. And vengeance."

His voice is bland. Neither vicious nor sly. It's nothing I can't agree with, yet all my arm hairs prickle.

"Fighting men should keep to fighting," I reply to the fire. "Let the saints do as they will."

Einion clears his throat. "This boy must recover. Bad enough that Gerald of Windsor got Llywelyn penteulu. Another one lost . . . Owain just . . . cannot have it." He leans close. "I've seen what you can do with those irons, and we'll all of us pray to Saint Elen."

I said I could save Owain's life. I promised it. I wept it, and it was Einion ap Tewdwr who pushed the brutes clear, who made them let me up, who hauled me staggering to Owain's side and stood over me blade in hand to see I made good that promise. That Owain survived at all was Saint Elen's doing as much as mine, for I could barely think—or breathe, or move— as I shuddered that knife clear. There can be no other reason I'd remember the time our best mouser limped into the steading with a gaping wound on his hindquarters, and my mother pressed a glowing-hot blade against the poor cat's side while he yowled and thrashed.

Rhys's eyes are shut tight, his jaw clenched. At midsummer, this boy was still eating his mother's oatcakes and tracking mud across her clean floor. I wrap my cloak around my hand and pull the spreader out of the fire. A faint whisper of steam curls off the blade. I nod to Einion, who secures Rhys's shoulder and wrist.

I have never once used the word *miracle,* but I can still hope for one. After all, that cat lived an age and caught mice under his big paws right up till his last days.

It's clear and cold and dizzyingly sunny. Margred and the cousins and I pile outside for a game, and we run up and down the courtyard kicking my ball and screeching like warbanders till our cheeks are burned pink and our feet sting from the ice. Finally, none of us can take another step, and we slump like dishrags on a bench outside the maidens' quarters, squinting against the sun-glint diamonds on what's left of the snow. Then the maids and nurses appear in the doorway, clucking over the girls' red toes and sighing mightily in my direction for winding them up before they have to sit for lessons. I assure the cousins I won't do anything fun without them, then promise to come by the maidens' quarters before supper.

Now I'm lurking in a dim corner of the hall, idly toying with my spindle while Owain and the lads are gathering at the door. They're going hunting, and they're daring one another not to wear undergarments, laughing and shoving like drunken halfwits.

The wives and sisters and mothers from the feast have drawn the hall benches near the hearth, and now they're chattering over their spinning and sewing in the gentle orange light. Isabel sits among them, giggling because of a knot in her yarn.

Rhael and I always talked about how it would be. We'd marry brothers two summers apart, just like us, and we'd have steadings across the vale and be in and out of each other's kitchens all the time.

Owain slaps Einion ap Tewdwr upside the head, and the lads cackle and mock him. I tease out a length of leader yarn, there in the corner by myself with my secondhand spindle.

Rhael and I each wanted two children, a son and a daughter, and they'd play together all day while we cooked and hauled and spun and laughed. Our husbands would come home from the high pastures, and we'd sing ballads and tell stories while the sun sank over the hills.

A shadow slants across my legs. Owain stands over me, cloak aswirl at his shoulders. "You all right, sweeting?"

I nod and show him the twist of thread around the spindle shaft.

"Aw, you don't want to sit on the floor all alone." He gestures cheerfully over his shoulder at the wives clustered near the hearth. "You were looking forward to meeting my stepmother, weren't you?"

I touch my arm where Cadwgan seized me, where Isabel

slid her cool fingers beneath his grip and pulled him clear. "My lord . . ."

"What?" Owain's smile drops abruptly. "Do you not want to pass the time with her?"

No. I don't. Not now.

Of course I can't say that, so I go limp and let Owain happily steer me across the hall like a sheepdog at the whistle. He pulls me to a halt at one end of their fortress of benches, nods graciously to Isabel, and drawls, "*Mama.* A pleasure, as always."

Isabel swats him playfully. "You wretch. Your mama clearly didn't take a switch to you enough."

"Hmm. No wonder you and my father get along so well." Owain nudges me forward and makes a show of kissing my cheek. "You remember Elen. She needs some company to spin with."

We may not be outsiders together, Isabel and I, but I can make a better showing. Especially here, among the wives. If she's decided we'll not be friends, at the very least I must keep her from becoming an enemy.

But while I flail for something to say—anything—that doesn't sound foolish or false, Isabel's impish smile goes bland and cold. "She can't sit here. You know what your father would say."

Oh saints. We would have been natural allies, but the only voice in her ear for two years has been Cadwgan's. Little wonder Isabel and I have never met properly.

"Whatever my father tries to tell you about Elen is unkind,

unwarranted, and profoundly untrue," Owain says, "especially for a man who thinks as highly of the saints as he does. Besides, we both know he's not happy if he's sparing the rod."

Isabel smirks and rolls her eyes good-naturedly.

"You, on the other hand, know how to hold out a proper welcome to your hearth." Owain bows his head again, and Isabel shrugs, coy and demure, but she can't quite hide her triumphant smile. "What'll people think if they see Elen sitting in the dust all alone? She is a guest in your hall, after all. She is *my* guest in your hall."

Isabel looks pained, but she sighs and points to an empty place at the end of the bench. I make no move. The wives busy themselves sewing or spinning, but they're watching us sidelong. Owain's attention is mostly over his shoulder near the door, where the lads are jostling and passing a flask and snickering. Only when he nudges me again do I perch on the very edge of the bench. It bites a sharp line into my backside. Once I'm seated, Owain grins, kisses me again, then leaves without a backward glance. He rejoins the lads, and they pile out the door and thrash their way outside, throwing snowballs, mayhap, as they head toward the gate.

I pinch out some wool like nothing is amiss and push the spindle down my leg to get a good twist. They're all watching me, and Owain loves it when people speculate. After several long moments, after the courtyard is quiet, Isabel clears her throat. "You must go."

"Beg pardon?" I widen my eyes, all innocence.

Isabel rises and jabs a finger at the corner where I came from, but I intentionally let my work tangle and then start fixing it. If I'm not on this bench when Owain returns, there'll be an argument I've no wish to be at the center of.

"Awww, leave the poor little lass alone." Gwerful tsks and pulls a stitch clear with plump fingers. "Owain will soon take a proper wife, and then where will she be? Out on her ear, that's where. Unless she starts giving him sons." She glances at me like I don't have the sense to work this out myself, but I can't think of sons without smelling smoke.

"I doubt it." Annes grins. "Whatever else, she's made Owain like her better than any of our husbands like us. Who knows? Mayhap she'll end up the proper wife."

The women giggle because it's hilarious that a girl born in some nameless steading might one day wed a king's son. I laugh, too, because I'm picturing the look on Cadwgan ap Bleddyn's face should such a thing somehow come to pass.

"If it were as easy as that, don't you think she'd have done it by now?" Eiluned picks a fleck of grime out of her wool. "I would have."

It's not a matter of easy. I wish it was. But it never will be.

"Come now, don't taunt her," Gwerful scolds. "She might stay kept, but Owain will marry a girl like Isabel here. Someone with land and a family full of sword-arms. Someone his father would have peace with."

"Poor child! At least the saints have blessed her—"

"Shut up, all of you!" Isabel snaps. "If my husband walks by and sees her here, I'll never hear the end of it. She may be a guest in my hall, but I do *not* have to pass time with her!"

I grip the bench edge, but Isabel wrenches me up, spindle and all, and shoves me hard. I stumble backward into a baby wobbling on tiny bare feet while clutching a fistful of his nurse's skirts. The baby loses his grip and sits down hard on his backside.

Miv.

Miv we hid in the shadows. Already she was crying in her cradle, arms up, *hold me hold me hold me.* Rhael said they would not care about her. Mam and Da would come back from the hills and find her wet and hungry and angry, but unharmed.

We did not think of fire.

This baby is not Miv. Miv had shaggy dark hair past her ears. This baby has a trace of sawdust-colored ringlets struggling free from a little gray hood. This baby looks up at me, up and up, and his lip trembles as he stretches his arms to be held.

An elbow hits my ribs, and I stagger, hard, crunching Gwerful's foot and knocking over Annes's sewing basket. When I recover, clutching my side, Isabel is drawn up like a murderess with the child on her hip.

"Did you just knock my baby down?" She strokes his tiny round cheek again and again. "You did. I saw you. Your master put you up to this, didn't he? Owain ap Cadwgan may be all smiles to my face, but I know exactly what he'd do to little Henry given half a chance. One more brother means his share of land and cattle is that much less, and don't think I haven't heard him calling my son a half-breed cur!"

I want to beg Isabel's pardon. I want to tell her my imposing on her spinning circle was not my idea, that she must pay Owain no mind for he's trying to needle his father through her. That no one put me up to anything, but they did, and Miv is wailing and Rhael stands chin up defiant for a staggering long moment before Einion ap Tewdwr roars like a beast and slings her against the wall, Owain at her feet with a knife-hilt beneath his arm.

I dodge around Isabel and throw myself out the main hall doors into eye-dazzling snow that stings my bare feet. I slog to the chapel, where Llywelyn penteulu's body still lies before the high altar.

I don't have a fire iron. I do have a meat knife.

I draw it warband-style, my thumb pressed to the tang like Owain taught me, but the moment I come within an arm's length of the body, I freeze.

Even now.

"Goddamn you," I mutter, and I swallow hard and grip the knife till it burns.

That first year, echoes of it happened right before my eyes, day after day, whenever Llywelyn penteulu entered the room, whenever I so much as heard his voice. I kept to the shadows and thought about knives and imagined this moment a thousand different ways.

It's been three summers now. Owain believes the playact like it's the paternoster and has not taken a proper wife. I can move from hearth to kitchen to spindlecraft, smile from my place at Owain's right hand, and sleep through the night.

I slack my grip, roll the knife-hilt in my hand, twice, thrice. Then I slam the blade into its sheath at my hip and turn away. I wouldn't be seeing echoes at all had Owain ap Cadwgan not led Llywelyn penteulu and the others to my steading. Had Owain not kicked in my door and let the wolves in behind him.

January 1110

†

EPIPHANY FINALLY COMES, AND THE DAY AFTER, WE
gather at barely-light in the yard. I'm bound for the hunting
lodge at Llyssun. Owain and his warband are headed south
toward Dyfed.

This part is always hard. I still get a bellyful of worms whenever Owain leaves on a raid, and I won't think of the body in the
chapel that'll go unburied till the ground thaws. As the priest
gives them a blessing, the lads stomp and shift against the cold,
their breath all in ghostly puffs. Among them is Rhys. He should
be near a fire with his wound bound up in damp cloth and a
mug of stew in his good hand, but instead he stands with the
others, bleary-eyed and pale. Not feverish, though. That's something, even if the bandages are a little grubby and he has politely
but insistently refused to let me look at the wound no matter
how I ask.

I did catch him in the chapel whispering thanks to Saint Elen. I overheard the word *miracle*. I went around smiling for days.

Margred comes onto the stoop of the maidens' quarters, sleep-tousled and wrapped in a nubby cloak that's too big for her. She holds up the toy mouse and waves its little paw.

I'll make her a dog next. It'll be Easter before we know it.

Owain steps out of the hall and into the knot of noblemen at the doorstep. His cousin Madog punches him cheerfully on the shoulder, and Owain nods. Madog leans over to whisper something in Owain's ear, but Owain steps a pace away.

Nearby there's a thrash and a scuffle and a throaty yelp. Einion ap Tewdwr has Rhys in a headlock, and Rhys is struggling like a madman to keep Einion's blade from his throat.

"Hey!" I blurt, and Owain turns just as Einion looses Rhys, who stumbles, clutching his arm, glaring.

"Sorry, lad," Einion says to Rhys as Owain storms up, Madog trailing him like a curious puppy. "You're not ready. Another fortnight for certain. Mayhap longer."

Owain squints at Rhys. "Let's see it."

"It's fine, my lord," Rhys mutters. "He just took me by surprise, is all."

"Oh, aye," Owain drawls, "and Normans are known for giving fair warning before they seize you and run you through. Show me your arm."

Rhys scowls but peels back the bandage enough to reveal

some of the wound. It's a dull red now, not bright blood-shiny, and the scab is no longer tender, but it's nowhere near healed. When Owain shakes his head, Rhys insists, "I'm sound! I'll not be so slow when there's Normans to kill."

"Perhaps," Owain replies mildly, "but it won't matter, for you'll be taking Elen to Llyssun."

Rhys gapes, first at Owain and then at me. The poor boy looks convinced he'll be my minder for the rest of his natural life while the grown-ups go out a-plundering. I'm delighted, though. It's several days' walk to Llyssun. I will ask Rhys how fares the arm. I'll recommend a salve. I'll remind him how close to death he came, how wound-sickness takes many healthy men to their graves but not him. He will mutter something and shake hair over his eyes, but he'll touch his bandaged wound like I'm blessed.

And I will forget for entire moments that the whole thing is merely a playact.

"I'd strongly recommend *shutting your mouth* and having a care what you say to me next," Owain says to Rhys in a steel-edge voice, "while you recall that the speed of your blade matters to more necks than just your own. I will not put a single man of my teulu at risk for the sake of one little pisser's pride."

Rhys flinches.

"Besides, I know you'd not want me to think that you object to seeing to Elen's safety like it's some kind of *chore*," Owain goes on, and Rhys squirms and studies his feet. "So off you go to Llyssun and let your arm heal. And don't worry. There'll be plenty of Normans for you to kill." He grins. "You have my word on that."

"Which brings us to the question of your penteulu." Madog claps Owain's shoulder again and smiles.

Margred's father holds a fort near Llyssun. Once Madog has been made penteulu, he's sure to let her come stay with me a while. We'll stoke a fire till it's very late. There'll be cider and giggling, and we'll play all the fortune-telling games we know.

Owain does not look at his cousin as he pushes Madog's hand off his shoulder with two fingers. "There's but one choice. It'll be Einion ap Tewdwr."

The lads raise a cheer, muss Einion's hair, shove him gleefully. Einion struggles for words, then remembers himself and kneels in the mud before Owain while muttering a jumble of gratitude and promises. Owain hauls him up by the forearm and cuffs him on the head, grinning.

"No," I whisper, because Einion ap Tewdwr has some unpleasant notions about saints and miracles and no sisters of noble birth who play at ball, and now he's at Owain's right hand.

"What the hell, Owain ap Cadwgan?" Madog growls.

"I'll tell you what the hell. While you were over there telling me why you should be penteulu, Einion was over here behaving like one."

"What has that to do with anything? I'm your first cousin! Our fathers were brothers!" Madog's hand quivers near his blade-hilt.

Owain makes a show of shrugging, and an uncomfortable silence falls over the yard. The lads have frozen mid-revel, and Einion stands to like a thief caught with four purses. In the doorway of the maidens' quarters, Margred looks ready to rush over and hug her brother fiercely and glare down anyone who'd say such things to him.

At length Madog asks, "You're really going to pass me over? Here? In the king's dooryard? In front of your warband?"

"I am."

Einion. Einion will be penteulu. Einion ap Tewdwr, who killed them both and seized all the beasts.

"And now that it's settled, we must be off." Owain nods at the gate. "Those goods won't plunder themselves, you know. Rhys, you've your orders. Einion, let's go."

Madog closes his mouth and squares up. "You're a bastard whoreson, Owain ap Cadwgan, and by God, I will *end* you."

Owain merely smiles and snaps off a taunting little wave, and at Einion's gesture the lads fall into their columns and march away, heading south. On his way past me, Owain falls out of line, slides his hands under my cloak, and pulls me close for a kiss. He glances one more time at Madog, now fully gripping his blade handle, grins, then glides after the lads.

I watch them till they're gone. Einion ap Tewdwr, of all men. Einion penteulu now.

It's not unheard of to name a penteulu who isn't a kinsman, but doing it when one stands fighting fit before you is meant to land and land hard.

"How's the wound?" I ask Rhys quietly, and I wait for him to touch the bandages.

"We should go," Rhys mutters, and nods at the gate in the same motion he shakes hair over his eyes. His face is still red, though whether that's from Einion's arm crushing his windpipe or being relegated as my minder I can't be sure.

On our way out, we pass Madog ap Rhirid muttering very black things to himself in the shadow of the wall. Any other time I wouldn't give two figs for his foul mood, but if I could change Owain's mind, I would. I thought to see Margred again at Easter, but now that she's the sister of a man Owain publicly snubbed instead of the sister of Owain's penteulu, it might be longer still.

RHYS SPENDS THE FIRST DAY OF THE TRIP CURSING in a low mutter and plowing a pace ahead just to make sure I know he's better than healthy. The second day he wordlessly walks at my side, and as evening is falling, he sidles up as we're about to raise camp. He holds out his injured arm, the bandages already unrolled.

He's been waiting to do this. Waiting till he's nowhere near anyone who'll call him pisser or ask if he's the kind of milk-sop who whines for his mama whenever he gets a little scratch. Rhys isn't showing me his wound because he thinks something's wrong. It's because he's four and ten, he's been six months away from home, and more than medicine or a miracle, this boy needs a bit of kindness that no one else will think to give him.

Rhys shakes long tangly curls over his eyes as I step near. There's a faint shadow of hair on his upper lip, and oh saints but four and ten is young. Younger even than almost-twelve, because Margred is still chasing butterflies and sneaking honey cakes and has not been asked to look terror in the eye.

Mayhap Rhael felt this way too when she told me not to be afraid.

"You'll be back among them before you know it," I tell him, and instead of whisking away like a cat, he smiles at the dirt and mutters his thanks, touching the raised edge of the wound as he kneels to kindle a fire.

†

WE ARRIVE AT THE HUNTING LODGE MIDMORNING.
It takes hardly any time to get things settled. The steward keeps
the place well in the absence of his lord. He's been in Cadwgan's
service so long he remembers Owain toddling around the place
in baby gowns. If he's not harried, the steward will tell stories
of tiny Owain pissing circles on the walls or trying to ride the
wolfhounds like ponies and getting bitten when they tired of it.

On my way into the hall I always pause before a series of
thigh-high gashes in the door frame where Owain's mother once
marked his height with her meat knife. I thumb each one in
order and wonder how she got him to keep still long enough to
get a good reckoning. Llyssun is my favorite of all the royal residences because it's got these small reminders that Owain's family
isn't always turbulent and complicated. There was once a place

for a mother who delighted in her growing son, so there's got to be a place for a girl who'd live beside him.

By day, the household is unremarkable. Servants move trestle boards and feed the hearth fire, children run around, and sleet drags against the walls like animal claws. By day I often forget for long stretches that Owain isn't here. It's like he's just out hunting with the lads and he'll be back for supper all bootsteps and off-color jokes, and later I'll follow him to the big bed in the king's chamber and drift to sleep curled beneath his arm.

It's when daylight starts to fade and there's no Owain that the quiet sets in. Not the restful kind of quiet, either. Not the quiet that comes with spinning in glowing firelight or petting a pup asleep across your knees or listening to your father and mother sing two-part ballads, their voices twining through the dark while you nestle deeper into your pallet with your sister's back warming yours.

It's the quiet that makes me force myself to eat supper all smiles because people are watching. The quiet that keeps me huddled in the big bed, cold and awake and alone. The quiet that makes me recall every time I thought of the knife, how easily I could have killed Owain ap Cadwgan and finished the work my sister started, and wonder why under Heaven I would do such a thing when I should be thanking Almighty God for him.

In that quiet, there are brothers two summers apart. The older one curls his lip in disgust while the younger one just looks sad. They fade into the hills like they never were, and I reach a hand across the expanse of bed to where Owain should be but isn't.

FEBRUARY 1110

OUT IN THE YARD, THERE'S A SERIES OF SHOUTS AND the scrunch of gate hinges, then Einion penteulu calling for the steward. I put aside my wool and stow my spindle hastily enough that I seem excited, but not urgent and panicked like there's cause for alarm. People are watching.

The lads flood the courtyard, plunder on their backs and on tethers behind them. Owain is cheerful and windblown atop a sleek black horse, wearing a crimson cloak he didn't leave his father's house with. There's not a scratch on him.

I turn my eyes Heavenward and silently thank Saint Elen and any other saint listening. Then I head across the yard to greet him — and see the girl.

She's older than me, likely a few summers older than Owain. Her honey-colored plait twists like a gallows rope over her shoulder, and she's wearing a bloodstained cloak cinched over a nightgown. Two little boys hunch at her side. One looks about six summers, the other mayhap three. The older boy glares mutinously while the younger looks ready to collapse.

I stop where I stand and turn openmouthed to Owain as he swings down from his horse. He grabs me at the waist and kisses me firm and fierce. He's cold from the wind, and his leather armor jabs me shoulder to hips.

Owain is talking, big and grinning and boastful. Normans running like frightened dogs. How they fell like ripe barley beneath his warband's blades. How everything burned so beautifully.

I can hardly draw breath. I can't look away from the girl.

"Gerald of bloody Windsor never saw us coming." Owain cranes his neck to peer into her face as she stares hard at the ground. "Did he, Nest?"

The girl, Nest, lifts her chin. "That's because I helped him escape the moment I heard your noise. All you've done is mark yourself. So don't ever stop looking over your shoulder, for my husband will not rest until your lifeless corpse is hanging from a tree for the ravens to feed on."

Husband. This is Nest ferch Rhys ap Tewdwr. Daughter of the king of a realm several years fallen. Wife of Gerald of Windsor. Standing in the courtyard of Llyssun, barefoot and in her nightgown.

"Oh yes," Owain taunts, "I'm terribly frightened of a coward whoreson who slid down the shit shaft to avoid facing me like a man."

They'll have rattled through her yard. Kicked in her door. Flooded through like blood from a wound. They'll have smashed the crockery and rifled through linens for hidden coins. Shoved anything valuable into purse or tunic.

Hard to the floor. Cold everywhere.

Nest grits her teeth as she tries to keep the younger boy on his feet. Then a baby begins to fuss, a low *weh-weh-weh* like the sound that used to wake me in the dim hours of the morning. Nest wearily shifts enough to heave a baby out of a sling beneath her arm and dark thatchy hair Miv I have to push the cradle against the wall I have to save Myfanwy —

But this baby is not Miv. It's not Miv because I left her behind to burn.

Owain is ordering Nest to take the children inside, but it's a slurry of sound because Rhael's shoulder presses against mine but it isn't, it can't be, it's years ago and it's yesterday and I'm up against the steading wall and already the room is filling with smoke.

"Sweeting? *Hey.*" A hand on my shoulder. Not rough, but insistent. Owain frowns at me.

"You . . ." I stay standing. Somehow.

"I said, help Nest with Gerald's brats." Owain glances with distaste at her as she wriggles the baby — *Not Miv* — into the older boy's arms.

Touch them. Warm and squirmy, smelling of porridge and soap. Not Miv. I left my sister behind.

Nest bends over the littler boy, who is curled like a dead grub at her feet, but the older boy is struggling to keep hold of Not Miv as she strains toward their mother. Nest scrabbles to catch the baby mid-tumble.

The littler boy blinks slow, his thumb wedged firmly in his mouth. In one fist is a ratty square of faded red cloth that he clutches against his chest. Miv would be this big. She's not, though. I left her to burn. To save my own skin.

I kneel and collect the smaller boy out of the mud. He's dead weight like a sack of barley when I heft him onto my hip. He drops his head on my shoulder and rubs the cloth against his cheek.

The older boy glares up at me. "Put my brother down or I'll hurt you."

"William, hssst!" Nest raps him upside the ear. "Not even this girl, do you hear? Not a word to *any* of these filthy brutes."

"Mama—"

"I said *hssst*. Mama needs to think." Nest presses a fist to her mouth, blinking, blinking.

"I'll not harm your brother," I reply quietly to William, "nor you. Nor your mam nor your . . . the baby."

William scowls and gestures at Owain. "*He* will."

I begin to tell the boy that he's a hostage, and hostages are kept comfortably and not harmed. They're held to guarantee the good behavior of an enemy, or traded for something valuable. There's no profit in doing violence to a hostage.

But hostages are not marched barefoot and taunted with a tale of their capture. They're not made to stand half-dressed and shivering in the midst of a warband.

So mayhap William ap Gerald and his siblings and his mother are not hostages. Mayhap that's not what Owain has in mind at all.

ONCE WE'RE IN THE HALL, I LEAD NEST AND THE
little ones toward the warm hearth and the cushioned benches
there. It's easily the most comfortable place in the hunting lodge,
but Nest veers toward a dark corner away from all the doors. As
I follow, the smaller boy lies heavy on my shoulder, his fingers
digging like talons.

In the corner, Nest drops to her knees, then collapses against
the wall and slides into a heap. The baby lands in her lap,
squealing joyfully like it's a game of horsey. Nest closes her eyes
and breathes out long and shuddery. When William burrows
against her, she hugs him close and holds on. Owain wouldn't
have made Nest walk the whole way, but one look at her cold-
reddened feet and I know she walked enough. Without a word,
I lower the younger boy next to her, and she chokes on a sob as
she holds him tight.

"Will you ask them to kill me first?" William whispers to his mother. "I don't want to watch you die."

"Shh, lambie. No one's going to die. Not you. Not David. Not Angharad." Nest pets his hair with one shaking hand. "Don't be afraid."

William scrubs his eyes with his wrist. David sucks his thumb while Not Miv squirms and fusses. Nest squints up at me, taking my measure. In a cool, courteous voice she says, "Thank you."

I nod. I look everywhere but her face. Owain ap Cadwgan did not kill the wife of Gerald of Windsor in the burning shadow of her home.

Instead he seized her. And her beasts.

I'm pressed into a corner of the chapel. Holding a fire iron in both hands and making myself breathe.

Killing Gerald of Windsor would have been one thing. Most of the Welsh kings and dozens of Norman border barons would have drunk Owain's health till the smallest hours, and even Gerald's so-called allies would have taken horse without delay to seize his lands and castles.

But Owain did not kill Gerald of Windsor. Instead he did something far worse.

Owain will feast his warband tonight and divide the plunder into shares. It will get loud and it will go late. By morning my hands must be empty. By morning I must be firmly here, at Llyssun. Nowhere else.

A shadow slants across the floor. Rhys shifts in the doorway, holding his wounded arm in a way he wishes looked healthy. I should ask about his injury to keep him in the habit of touching that healing scar. I can't, though. I can't think beyond the cold metal in my hand.

"Ah . . . it's coming on suppertime."

"Already? Well. Doesn't matter. I'm not hungry."

"My lord says to bring you." Rhys clears his throat. "Now."

I tighten my grip and cut a glance at him, but his cheeks are pink and he's toeing the floor.

Loud and late it is, then. At least they'll be in good humor. Safely returned, the lot of them, with treasure for every man. As if Saint Elen herself saw to it.

The first place we go is the kitchen, where Rhys watches as I hand over the fire iron. He stays a generous armslength from me all the while. Once it's done, I lace my hands together to keep them from feeling too empty.

In the hall, the steward is in heated conversation with Owain, who's lazily sipping from a mug. The steward stabs a finger at the corner where David lies wide-eyed and unmoving across Nest's lap and Not Miv is fighting William as he tries to keep her close. It's plain what the steward is saying—a king's son has no business shaming hostages with such callous treatment, and Owain should know better.

Owain glances at Nest where she sits like a toadstool, hunched and unmoving, still in her nightgown with her hair straggling loose from its braid, and he grins. The steward's face is growing red, but he bows curtly and strides away before one of the fists clenched at his sides gets the better of him.

Rhys nudges me. I've stopped walking, and I'm near enough to the corner that William looks up at me, lost and floundering: *Please just make it better.* I stumble forward. Away from them. Toward Owain, who takes my hand, puts it on his arm, then calls out to the hall, "Nest will play at kitchen maid."

Nest's jaw drops, her mouth moving soundlessly. At length she shifts David onto the floor and claws her way to her feet. She squares up like a warbander and says, quiet but clear, "Not even you would dare treat a hostage this way, Owain ap Cadwgan."

Owain lifts a brow. "Who said you were a hostage?"

"I'm a *slave,* then?"

He flicks his fingers at the hall door, offhand, careless, like the half command is all that's needed. Nest takes a slow measure of the room. The lads cackling and tipsy, clustered, watching her over mug rims. The steward long gone and hobbled besides. Me—her eye glides over me like I'm a mongrel dog Owain holds on a tether. At last she hauls David and William each to his feet, then shoulders Not Miv.

"And where might you be taking your sons, Nest, wife of Gerald the Coward? Into the kitchen?" Owain tsks. "However do the Normans produce fighting men?"

"I'll not leave them here alone," Nest replies through her teeth. "If you want to kill them, you'll do it looking into my eyes."

William makes a tiny animal sound and pulls his cloak over his head.

Owain puts on a look of great hurt. "They're just little babies, Nest. What kind of beast do you take me for?"

Nest wisely presses her lips together, though it's clear she'd sorely like to tell him just what kind of beast she takes him for.

"I'm really just a lamb," Owain goes on in a voice of butter. "Elen will tell you. Won't you, sweeting?"

Owain pulls me onto the bench at his right hand, harsh and sudden, and grins at Nest, all teeth. She blinks rapidly. I know exactly what she sees. What he'd have her see. His hand on my arm and me all but on his lap. I dare not shake him off or shift away, but I cannot look at her, either.

Nest takes her time hefting David onto one hip while settling Not Miv on the other, and she herds a whimpering, limping William in front of her toward the hall door.

There are hostages at royal residences all the time, sons and brothers of men Cadwgan can't quite bring himself to trust. They're given the best lodging the place affords, and they sit at table and go to mass with the rest of us. All that's denied them is freedom to come and go. Anything less, and Cadwgan's sons and brothers, and those of his allies, will get the same at someone else's hands.

The lads take their places at the trestle table, crowding the benches and elbowing one another. They're recounting the raid on Gerald of Windsor's home. How they went over the wall in the darkest part of night. How you could see the burning wreckage from leagues away till dawn and then some. What each of them took. Who each of them killed. Just like any ordinary raid. Only it's not.

At length — at *long* length — Nest shuffles into the hall with an earthenware bowl of something steaming. The lads chortle and laugh and hoot, and color swarms up her neck as she brings the bowl toward the king's chair and Owain, who's leaning his chin on one fist and regarding her with a faint taunting smirk.

Somewhere outside, Not Miv is wailing.

Nest places the bowl before Owain. Her eyes are steady but absolutely violent, and her hand trembles as if she'd like nothing better than to dump it in his lap. But she steps away. Bows her head.

"And the lads?" Owain asks in a loud voice.

Nest makes an incredulous gesture at them all, arrayed like a small army along the benches.

"It's a *great* honor, Gerald's wife, to serve such company at table." Owain smiles again, and I think of the knife, how there have been times I could have killed him in two simple moves. How he shouldn't even be alive, but he's alive because of me.

"I'll help her," I say quietly, and Nest is suddenly hopeful, all the way pleading even though I know what it must cost her to plead in this place, before them, even with me. I move to rise, but Owain grabs my arm hard enough to hurt and yanks me down with a rump-bruising thud.

"You will *not*."

Nest waits, pausing heartbeat after heartbeat, but I cannot pull free and swear that Saint Elen will turn her back on him for such deeds. That there will be no miracles if this is what he does with her blessing.

I have not hated Owain ap Cadwgan for a long time, but I hate him now.

Nest snorts and shakes her head slow like I'm a bag of flour weighted false with stones. She turns on her heel and trudges out of the hall.

"Your coward husband ran a lot faster than that!" Owain calls after her, and the lads laugh like madmen.

After a while Nest reappears, bringing more portions. The proper servants crowd the doorway for a peek at a highborn lady being made to do their work. The steward is among them, stiff and frowning, apparently convinced that silent fatherly dis-approval will mean something to Owain. The lads snicker and jeer as Nest moves among them. More than one has himself been a hostage, yet they pull her hair and slap her backside and step on her hem to trip her up. Hot stew slops over her wrists, leaving angry red welts and spattering her cloak and nightgown. The lads knew from the moment this meal began that something was different.

Mayhap they knew from the moment Owain kicked in her door.

I push a spoon through my stew. Spoons are not sharp, but I could make one so. At my elbow, Owain takes his supper and drinks his ale and presides over the goings-on with a smug, tri-umphant smile.

———◆———

It's well past supper. The trestle planks have been stacked against the wall, and the lads have grown bored and tired, departing one by one out to their lodgings and bedrolls. Nest hasn't returned from the kitchen.

Owain catches Rhys on his way out. "Go fetch her."

At supper Rhys carried on with the rest, but now he drags out the hall door like he's made of lead.

It's a freezing walk across the yard to the king's chamber. I'm pulling up my hood and wrapping my hands, hoping someone remembered to leave a hot brick to warm the bedclothes, when I realize Owain's not doing the same. He's leaning against the wall, arms folded, patient.

I have no liking for this.

Rhys swings the door open and Nest all but falls inside, Not Miv tucked in the sling at her middle. William stumps behind his mother, bent over from carrying David on his back. Nest heads right for the corner but freezes when she spots Owain waiting there. Then she backs to the nearest wall, pulling her sons with her.

"Will I want to post a guard?" Owain asks her.

Nest shakes her head once, curtly. "I'm no fool. I'm not going anywhere."

I tried it once. Not a threemonth after being marched away. I didn't pack anything. I didn't make a plan. I waited until the lot of them were asleep, then I got dressed and fled. I hadn't made it five arrowshots when Einion ap Tewdwr found me, and it wasn't even full dawn.

Owain dismisses Rhys with a single gesture. Rhys is out the door before Owain's hand falls still, and the latch snicks closed like a stone in a washtub. Then Owain rocks away from the wall. I move to his elbow, but he does not look at me.

"Your every act against me will come back to you." Nest lowers Not Miv to the floor and steps in front of her. "You'll pay a steep enough price for all you did at my home. Mercy serves you better now."

"I do not show mercy to Normans," Owain replies, "nor do I expect it from them."

"I am not Norman!" She flings a hand. An empty hand. "My father was once king of Deheubarth. My mother was kin to the king of Gwynedd. Two of the kingdoms of Wales. Two! I am one of your own. I am not your enemy!"

"No," Owain agrees quietly. "*You* are not my enemy."

I put a hand on Owain's arm. He shakes me off like a wet dog and reaches for Nest's wrist, and I am shoulder-to-shoulder with Rhael and my sister is about to die.

William plows toward Owain, a little blur of fists and cursing in two languages. Owain swivels and snares him by the hood, hoisting him off the ground so he dangles like a cat by the scruff. A dark stain spreads down the boy's hose. Nest is between them in an instant, throwing her weight on Owain's outstretched arm, worming both hands into Owain's grip on William's hood.

"Don't you dare hurt my children," she growls, but her voice breaks and she rasps, "Please, oh God, please, if there's any mercy in you!"

Owain looses William not quite gently and the boy staggers away several paces. He's choking on big quiet sobs, his hands over his head like the sky is falling. Nest moves toward her son, but Owain leans close to her ear and mutters something. I only catch *in front of your children.*

Nest blinks and blinks, presses a hand to her forehead. "All right, you bastard. If that's how it's going to be. All right."

When Owain gestures toward the hall door, toward the king's chamber beyond, she walks ahead of him without a word.

And then they are gone.

I'm on the floor. The whole room is blurry. A boy crouches nearby, curled up tiny. He reeks of piss. He's crying.

William. William ap Gerald, who even now pays for the sins of his father.

I crawl near. Hold out an arm to hug him. He'll push me away. Bid me leave him be. I can't help it, though, and I gently put a hand on his back. With a sob, William snakes his arms around my waist and grips tight like he might fall. I pull him close and pet his hair like I saw Nest do, like I once did with Miv, like I still sometimes do with Margred, and after a while his sobs wear down to heavy, snuffly breathing.

"Is . . ." William swallows. "Is he going to kill my mama?"

I shake my head. My throat feels full of wet sand.

"I hate him," the boy mutters. "My papa will kill him when he comes to save us."

Fled down the privy shaft. Deep in Dyfed by now, cowering

behind sturdy walls. I wonder if there's any truth to it or if it's spun of pure falsehoods. Gerald of Windsor is still alive, though, and by no means is it mischance. Nest said she helped him escape, but if Owain wants a man dead, he's soon dead. Gerald has no doubt as to who raided his house. Knowing whose warband has unmanned you is meant to linger like a bad smell. By now Gerald has learned what befell his wife and children, and it won't be long before he hears how Nest is anything but a hostage here. All because he ran like a rabbit to save his own skin.

We pushed Miv's cradle against the wall. We wanted her out of sight, so even if they did care about her, perhaps they would not see her.

"I wish Papa was here right now." William's voice is barely a whisper.

"I-I'm here," I reply quietly, because I am pushing down echoes one by one.

"He'll kill us, too." William's eyes are huge and staring in the dying firelight. "Me and David and Angharad. He'll kill us all dead."

This poor child believes it like gospel. He has no reason not to. And I have no reason to doubt Owain's willingness to leave each of them hanging from trees like a trail of breadcrumbs for Gerald of Windsor to follow.

"Hey." I gently move William's head so he's looking at me. "I know you're scared. I'm sorry for it. But you must keep your wits. All right? You can come out of a lot of things if you steady yourself."

William bites his lip. "You sound like Alice. Are you our new Alice?"

"I . . . I'm Elen."

"Mama said Alice had to stay behind," he goes on quietly, "but she wasn't moving when they made us leave."

I will not think how Einion penteulu bragged at supper about a baby nurse and how she wept and pleaded, the color Nest turned, how the others snickered as she fought to keep from being sick. I will not think of the door to the maidens' quarters, how it wouldn't withstand a single boot to the cross braces.

Instead I say to William, "Let's get you cleaned up."

He nods but makes no move, so I help him peel off his piss-soaked hose and give him a damp cloth to wash his legs. After a few half-hearted swipes, he drops the rag and wriggles back against me without a word. I collect David under my other arm. He lies against me like a toy stuffed with sawdust, and William reaches across my lap to push hair from his brother's eyes.

That leaves Not Miv. She's playing with a set of metal rings that I've seen the steward's grandson with.

The last time I held my baby sister, I had her on my hip as I slung the leather bucket dripping and heavy up the creek-ward path for what felt like the hundredth time that day. It did not occur to me to look over my shoulder or I might have seen the thin whispers of black smoke hovering over the next vale. I merely set the bucket by the fire and put Miv in her cradle with a wooden spoon to gnaw. I turned away from her, rubbing my sore arm and thinking how glad I was that it would be Rhael's turn to carry her next time.

I grab Not Miv under the armpits, tuck her into the crook of my leg, then whip my hands away. My palms are sweaty. My heart racing. But she doesn't cry. She doesn't judge me, cold and silent. All she does is drool and bang one ring on another with her little unburned hands.

I close my eyes. I told William I was here, and here's where I'm going to stay.

†

WHEN I AWAKEN, NEST IS STANDING OVER ME WEAR-
ing a servant's linsey gown. I startle and try to get up, but
William is fused to my side with both arms around my waist.
David is curled next to me, and Not Miv lies across my lap.

Nest will be seeing the mongrel dog off its tether. Near her
children.

But she sways on her feet. Her hair is loose and stringy, and
all she does is hold out her arms like she's waited an age to do it.
I lift Not Miv off my lap, and Nest takes her quick and hugs her
hard, one hand on the baby's head like she's newly born.

I gently peel William's arms away and slide out from under
both him and David. My sleeve is wet from where Not Miv
pissed on me sometime in the night.

"They're all right?" Nest does not look away from her sons
sleeping in a pile, like puppies.

I nod. I roll my aching shoulders and rub my neck.

"You're sure?"

"I sat with them all night."

Nest lets out the longest breath and slides down the wall in small, painful movements.

The hall is dim and still. No trestles being set up for a meal. The fire confined and austere. The steward is telling Owain not so subtly that he'll no longer find this fort comfortable, which means we're leaving and soon.

The door is open, though, probably left that way by Nest, and outside, Owain moves past in his leather armor, swearing and calling for Einion penteulu to make sure the lads are ready to leave before sunup.

William shifts in his sleep, one hand flailing until it falls on David. He curls close to his brother, his arm across the younger boy's shoulders. I kneel to retuck his cloak around them like I would for Margred, but Nest makes a fierce little noise in her throat. I pull my hand back. She says nothing else, only fixes me with a steady, narrow-eyed stare.

I am out the door. I don't even close it behind me.

In the yard, I soak the sleeve of my gown in the horse trough to be rid of the piss smell. The shock of cold water wakes me up right and proper, enough to reckon how much my belly hurts. It's good that the warband will spend the day on the march. I'm not sure I can be around Owain ap Cadwgan today.

Nest, either.

This won't be the first time we've left somewhere in a rush

with no breakfast, but when I turn up at the back door of the kitchen, the steward fills my apron with oatcakes and cheese. I nod when he says I'd best make sure it gets to the *right people*. I don't know how to tell him Nest wouldn't take the keys to Heaven from my rotting corpse.

Outside, under the kitchen's overhang, I shiver and fidget in the biting wind. My rucksack is in the hall. Where Nest is. Where the little ones are. But I've got to pack. I know better than to slow the warband down.

The children will drag the pace, though. They can't help it.

I'm rushing across the yard and dodging patches of muddy ice and worrying about the little ones when I almost collide with Owain, blocking the hall door. His back is to me, and he's leaning on the frame and shaking his head in an overdone way at whatever's going on inside. I duck under his arm and my stomach clenches.

In the corner, Nest is trying to get David to stay on his feet, but Not Miv on her shoulder keeps pushing and struggling to reach the ring toy lying nearby. William tugs her cloak and whines that he's hungry and he needs to piss and his feet hurt. Some of the lads are here—Rhys, and Morgan and Llywarch, and Einion penteulu, all eating cold oatcakes and hulking like wolves and watching the show.

Nest does not want my help. She has little reason to trust me and less reason to want my company. Owain made very sure of that.

"Look at them all," Owain muses, "Gerald's three little

bratlets, clamoring like pigs at a trough. They all have the misfortune to take after him, too. Every time I look at them, I see their whoreson coward father."

Nest straightens and knuckles tears out of her eyes. "Whatever this is, I'll not go along with any of it. So kill us, damn you. Kill us and be done with it."

William freezes. I can't stop myself from moving a few paces so I'm nearer to him, and he grapples a handful of my cloak like it'll save him somehow.

Owain shrugs elaborately. "Had I planned to kill you, you'd be dead now, but I can be done with you if that's what you want. You're welcome to stay here in my father's fort with all his men. Gerald's brats, though? They'll come with me."

"You son of a—" Nest bites it back. "No. You wouldn't dare."

Owain gestures, and Einion penteulu wrenches William clear of me so hard and sudden that a scrap of my cloak tears away in his hand. William lets out a pig-slaughter shriek and goes limp under Einion's grip. I leap toward David, scooping him up and pressing his face into my neck. The little boy is gasping silent, shuddery sobs, and when Einion penteulu reaches his free hand toward David, I bare my teeth at him, and he stops where he stands.

Nest stumbles back, clutching the baby, but Morgan seizes her shoulder and waist and holds her fast. Jostled, Not Miv begins to howl. Owain watches without expression as Nest wrenches and twists and swears like a fighting man; then he gestures to Rhys.

When Rhys grapples Not Miv around the middle, Nest screeches, "Stop! Stop this right now, damn you! Just stop it!"

David is heavy in my arms. William still clings to the raggedy strip of my cloak like it anchors him to shore, whimpering with every unsteady breath he draws.

"You're ready to behave, then?" Owain asks Nest. "Both you and Gerald's brats? Best decide now. It's not a chance you'll have twice."

Nest nods fierce and knobby, like it hurts her neck to do it and she can't trust her voice with it. "You'll be sorry before this is over, Owain ap Cadwgan."

"I doubt that." Owain nods to Morgan and he lets her go. Then Owain aims a knuckle at Nest and says, "Get Gerald's brats into the yard. We've a lot of ground to cover."

Nest sinks against the wall, patting Not Miv absently. She's still panting like a hound in August, breath after shuddering breath. Einion penteulu looses William, and the boy stumbles into me. I expect him to push past and flee to his mother, but instead he presses his snotty face into my side, hiccoughing and shaking. I put an arm over his shoulders and hold him close.

"Mayhap Saint Elen will whisper in their little ears," Einion says in a silky voice that makes me want to kick him where it counts, "and get them to behave the way she says to."

"Owain wants the little ones ready to travel," I reply, "and after that spectacle, it'll go easier if none of you lot are here."

Einion penteulu snorts, but he gestures to the others and follows Owain into the yard, where the lads will be gathering. Nest and I are left looking at each other in the empty hall. In the silence, I shift David to my other hip, then pull a broken piece of oatcake out of my apron and hand it to Not Miv. She gnaws it around whimpering cries.

I wait for Nest to square up and coldly tell me to go away, but instead she asks quietly, "What are you?"

The patter rises to save me, but the well-trod line that I'm Owain's protector and bring him the blessing of a saint won't impress this woman. In fact, it's more likely to make her start planning how she might cut my throat and use my corpse as a stepstool, the more easily to cut Owain's as well.

So I flail. I stammer. I pet David's hair and cast about for something to tell her.

"She's Elen," William says to his mother, "and she found me new hose to wear even though they're too big and she found Angharad a spoon to chew 'cause of her toothing. And mayhap she can be our new Alice since the old one—"

"Hsst." Nest scrubs her free hand over her upper arm where Morgan held her. Her lips keep moving though she makes no sound.

I shift David again. He's heavy, but I make no move to put him down. Nest wanted none of this. It won't take much more for her to fall apart completely. I can hold her mistrust against her, or I can hold out a hand.

I know very well which Owain ap Cadwgan would prefer.

"I could help you with them." I say it gentle and comforting, like when Margred was upset after one of the cousins called her a baby because her ears weren't pierced. "On the walk. If you want me to."

"On the walk," Nest echoes softly, and she looks down at her linen-wrapped feet and the tipped-over benches.

"But we need to go." I nod toward the hall door.

Nest opens her mouth to say she can't. Not another step, not on fitful rest and without a crumb of breakfast.

That's when William seizes his mother's hand and pulls her stumbling over to me. Then he takes my hand too, smiling bravely up at each of us in turn.

WE WALK NORTHWARD IN SILENCE, ME WITH DAVID on my back, Nest with Not Miv in the sling, and William at my side or trailing behind. Owain is moving deeper into the kingdom of Powys, and if Gerald of Windsor thinks to follow, he'll look over both shoulders with every step.

Near midmorning, Nest clears her throat and leans close so William can't overhear. "Tell me truly. What does he plan to do with my children? Please just say it plain. Even if it's bad. I must ready myself. I'll not give him that, too."

"Depends." I kick a rock and add softly, "Depends on you."

"Does that mean they're safe, then? As long as I do as I'm bidden?" Nest's voice goes cold. "Because if they're dead either way, there's no profit in me behaving."

No one notices women in the shadows. No one believes they will bring down the dagger.

I tread carefully. "You heard Owain. If he wanted you dead, you'd be dead. He's a lot of things, but he's not a liar."

"Killing me gets Owain ap Cadwgan his precious vengeance once. Keeping me alive means he can take his vengeance at his will, before all the Norman border lords and Welsh kings. My husband, too." Nest curls her lip. "I'm worth something to him, at least. That means my children are as well."

I nod. Being worth something to Owain ap Cadwgan is how you stay alive around him.

"All right, then," Nest murmurs. "I'll do as I'm told. For them. Until my husband negotiates our release, or kills that wretch and takes us back."

If, I want to say. Not *until.* It does not do to underestimate Owain ap Cadwgan.

But she walks beside me calmer now, steadier, like there's a point to doing it after all, so I shuffle David higher on my back and say nothing.

†

By nightfall, we're settled into a cozy fort near a stream, one with a steward whose opinions can be swayed with gifts. Owain feasts his warband and hands out more plunder from the raid on Gerald of Windsor's home. He makes Nest sweat over the meal and serve them at table again, but this time she does it serenely, without a whisper of rage. Owain watches her calm, graceful movements with a faint scowl. As Nest moves past with a brimming water basin, he pushes his knife off the trestle. "Gerald's wife, pick that up."

Nest sets the basin on the table. As she kneels, Owain dumps the murky water over the edge, soaking the front of her gown. The thin garment clings to her, and the lads get an eyeful. They approve. Noisily and with vulgarity that tips the scales even for them.

I fidget in my seat at Owain's right hand. After the laughter and hooting dies down, I mutter, "I'm not feeling well. May I leave?"

"Supper will help," Owain replies. "Sit and eat, sweeting."

"It would truly do me good to lie down."

"Later. I would miss your company too much."

My belly really does hurt. The little ones are nowhere in sight. Chances are good they're in the kitchen with no one watching over them. Owain knows this, too. So I stay at my place. I think of the knife.

I'm eating my way through a slab of mutton and a massive wedge of honey cake when Owain slides an ornate bracelet made of twined silver over my wrist. He grins and squeezes my hand. I smile and thank him. I will wear it for a se'ennight, then I will put it with the others at the bottom of my rucksack. I am no longer four and ten, and foolish enough to believe these gifts mean something.

Owain calls for more wine. Nest comes by and pours, but her hand jerks, and she sloshes it over the table. Without thinking I begin to mop it up, but Owain tilts his head and tries to catch Nest's eye. "Such a fumble-fingers."

"Beg pardon," she mutters.

"Are you in some sort of distress?" Owain draws the last word out like a taunt.

"No, I'm fine." Nest takes the rag from me and swipes it across the table while trying not to glance at my wrist.

"This is yours," I blurt, holding up my arm so the bracelet slides toward my elbow.

Nest blinks rapidly and doesn't deny it.

"Your vile husband has a good eye for trinkets at least," Owain says.

"Gerald didn't give me that," she mumbles. "My father did."

I will not think of my father, how he'd bring Rhael and me armloads of flowers from the high pastures for us to weave into crowns. I strip the bracelet off my wrist and slap it into Nest's palm.

"Hey!" Owain grabs for the bracelet, but Nest steps away and holds it close to her heart. Then he turns on me and says, cold and level, "Do you value my gifts so little that you toss them away without a care?"

"No." I'm trembling. "But if you give me something, it becomes mine. Doesn't it? Can I not give away something of my own freely?"

Before Owain can respond, Nest slams the bracelet on the table in front of me, picks up the flagon, and moves away without a word. It's too late, though. He got to her and they both know it.

Owain slides the bracelet back onto my wrist. "You pity her. That's your concern. She will get no comfort here, though. Am I clear?"

I trace a finger over the silver twists and curves. I can't tell him that Saint Elen said if he must hold Nest and the little ones, he should keep them as proper hostages, comfortably and courteously.

"I have no liking for any of this," I reply.

"If it's not cruel and ugly, it won't be vengeance. I won't beg anyone's pardon for that." Owain takes a drink. "I do regret it bothers you, though. I haven't seen you smile since the Christmas feast."

I did smile then. I smiled when Owain taught his small swaggering cousins how to curse in French and when I bit into my slice of New Year cake and found the lucky coin. I grinned like a victorious warband chief when Margred told her mother she'd rather have her childhood nurse around another year instead of getting a proper lady's maid.

But I also smiled when Cadwgan floated his doubts and when Isabel crossed the yard to avoid me. I smiled when every noble in the hall drank the memory of Llywelyn penteulu and when their wives talked about me in my presence like I was a horse or a coffer.

"You're not"—Owain cocks his head—"*jealous*? Of Nest? And what I'm doing? Are you?"

We pushed Miv's cradle into shadow. Owain was first through the door. He glanced thrice around the steading, then went straight for Rhael.

I spin the bracelet on my wrist.

"Sweeting, come here."

Owain holds out an arm, and I hesitate only the smallest

moment before I slide over. He squeezes me tight and kisses my hair. "It's purely vengeance, I promise. The uglier it is, the faster Gerald of bloody Windsor will be spurred to rescue them. Word of how I'm treating her will reach him soon if it hasn't already. Every day that slips by and he can do nothing for her will make him more beast than man. So when he does come, he'll come raging, heedless, hellbent—and we'll be ready, the lads and I."

Owain grins, and I go cold. Gerald of Windsor will be dead, and Nest and the little ones will still be here. Which means no ransom. Which means no rescue. Which means neither Nest nor her children will any longer be worth anything at all to Owain ap Cadwgan.

THE FEAST IS INTO ITS SECOND DAY WHEN THE HALL
doors fly open loud enough to echo. The lads are none too steady
on their feet after barrels of wine and mead, and Owain actually
stumbles over the bench when he rises, dagger in hand. We're
not under attack, though. Attack would be considerably better
than Cadwgan ap Bleddyn storming down the aisle, scattering
hapless servants and shouting, "Christ Almighty, boy, tell me it's
not true!"

Owain flops back into the king's chair and stabs up some
mutton. "It's lovely to see you too, Da. So lovely that I'll forgive
the insult of you kicking in the door and coming armed into
this house."

"First of all, it's *my* house! I'm not yet dead enough for you
to be claiming royal residences beyond a few nights' lodging!

Besides, I'll be damned if I'll hear *any* of your smart mouth right now. Not when you've just kicked a hornets' nest."

Cadwgan scours the hall. All I'm doing is holding a flagon of wine while David and William cling to the ends of my cloak, but even so, I keep very still. Then he spots Nest in a corner, barefoot, half-dressed in a stained servant's gown, holding a fussing Not Miv to her shoulder. His mouth falls open and he stammers, "Christ on the Cross. It's worse than I thought."

Owain's face hardens. "Gerald of Windsor pays every day for the death of Llywelyn ap Ifor."

David tugs on my hem. He holds up his arms, eyes huge. I swing him onto my hip, and he burrows close.

"Son, Llywelyn ap Ifor was a good man, but this war was never meant to satisfy your need for vengeance. You were to leave Dyfed a smoking ruin and *undermine* whoresons like Gerald of Windsor!"

"I *did* leave Dyfed a smoking ruin." Owain grins. "And I've been undermining Gerald of Windsor by much more . . . thorough means."

"You must return Nest to her husband," Cadwgan growls. "Send her and the children home under safe conduct this afternoon."

Owain leans back in the massive carved chair. "I don't think I'll be doing that."

"I think you will." Cadwgan is fighting for calm. "This is Nest. She is the daughter of a Welsh king of an old and proud lineage. She is the wife of Gerald of Windsor, who holds a province that is *right on our southern border* for the English king — a man who considers Gerald a very close friend. If that wasn't enough, she bore the English king a son, for Christ's sake!"

"From what I hear, that's true of half the girls in England," Owain says with a smirk, but I suck in a breath, because if Gerald of Windsor and the English king have a common cause beyond ambitions toward Cadwgan's realm or outrage at the burning of Dyfed — and if that common cause is a king's honey-haired daughter both of them have lain with and have sons with — Saint Elen just may have finally lost patience with me and my foolish little playact once and for all.

"How do you think Gerald got to be a friend of the king?" Cadwgan makes a frustrated gesture. "The better Gerald keeps her, the higher the king's opinion of him. Damn you for a fool!"

"I was overcome by her charm," Owain replies, expressionless.

Cadwgan sighs impatiently. "If Gerald doesn't get her back soon, the English king could use this affront as just cause for an invasion. He could force me to submit and accept him as my overlord — or worse, install some Norman freebooter on the make to govern my kingdom. Gilbert fitz Richard de Clare would very much like to be a friend of the king, and he has thirty land-hungry knights at his command who've all been promised a piece of your patrimony."

Killing Gerald of Windsor would have been bad, but men die in raids, and the English king would have ranted a while before pulling another man from obscurity and giving him Dyfed to hold, giving him Nest in marriage so she'd be looked after. Just as he did with Gerald of Windsor all those years ago.

"If Gerald wants them back, he can come bareheaded up that aisle and beg for them on his knees." Owain takes a drink of wine. "Until then, I'll keep them as I see fit."

William twists a hand into my cloak and whispers, "Is my papa coming?"

I give him what I hope is a reassuring smile and put a finger to my lips because there's no good answer to that question.

"This is a mistake, son." Cadwgan shakes his head. "I'm as happy as you to see Gerald humbled, but this is beyond Gerald now."

"You worry overmuch. Everything's in hand." Owain rises from the king's chair and gestures grandly to it. "Take some meat? You must have been all day in the saddle."

"We're not done here," Cadwgan replies, but he lowers himself into the chair with a groan as Owain takes a seat on the bench next to him.

They'll want wine, and anything I can do to keep this fragile peace will be good for all of us. I gently pull away from William, hold up the flagon by way of explanation, and murmur that he should help his mother with the baby. He nods and creeps along the wall toward Nest, keeping to shadows. I approach the high table, David still on my hip, and fight down the desire to brain Owain ap Cadwgan with the flagon and knock half a measure of sense into him.

I made Owain this way, though. I stood over his sickbed and

taught it to him chapter and verse as I put salve on the raised ripple of flesh that my sister gave him and I burned clean.

"What does your oh-so-clever bedmate think of your captive?" Cadwgan asks Owain. "Are they tearing each other's hair out? Or mayhap you should be worried they're in league against you."

Owain laughs and holds up his mug. "Why would they be in league against me?"

I pour the wine, a long crimson sluice that catches stray winks of firelight.

"This isn't the first time Nest has been carried off by an enemy," Cadwgan says. "She had about eight or nine summers when the Normans killed her father and took her away to England. You came by your clever bedmate much the same way."

"It's nowhere near the same." Owain takes a drink and smooths a hand over my hip, and I twitch as if stung. "Elen saved my life. I keep her close. All the Normans did for Nest was shove her at the English king to help her get on in the world. Giving that roaming-handed lecher a child set her up for life."

That's one way to see it. How a man would see it.

Cadwgan frowns. "I don't think you understand the scale of what you've done. I planned a war, lad. Not a slaughter."

"I know exactly what I've done," Owain replies. "I've sent a message to every man the length and breadth of the kingdoms of Wales: Keep your damn hands off my birthright. Stay well clear of anything belonging to me and mine."

"That may be what you *think* you've done." Cadwgan tips his mug at Owain. "Gerald of Windsor will come for her, though. That means he's coming for you. No quarter given."

I will not think of my father, how he was killed with my mother and all the beasts seized so there was no one to come for me.

Nest's father, too. I touch the bracelet, then pull my sleeve over it.

Owain merely smiles and asks politely after Isabel's health. For a long moment Cadwgan looks capable of killing his son with his bare hands, then he coughs the kind of helpless laugh you do when there's nothing left to say.

Because when Gerald of Windsor comes for us, it won't be the hellbent, rage-driven attack of a mad dog after all. Not if Gerald can trade on his friendship with the English king. He'll call up an army of big Normans and use all the resources of Dyfed to hunt down the man who abducted and misused his wife and children.

Owain will have just the lads of his warband. And the favor of a saint he's never had a reason to question.

The feast peters out and Cadwgan leaves, but the lads still sit around the hall and laugh too loudly and tell boastful stories while drinking through the contents of Cadwgan's storehouse. Owain has had way too much wine and he's ignoring me to listen to Einion penteulu recount for the hundredth time today the bit about Gerald of Windsor escaping his home down the privy shaft, and I'm beginning to seriously question the spinning of that story. They'll be at it all afternoon and well into the evening. Most of the morrow as well. All of them together tight around the hearth, shoulder to shoulder, reliving every clunk of steel and firebrand-crackle and plundering of some precious thing. Rhys holds a mug with his good hand, and with his other lifts a bucket of water up and down, up and down, so the muscles relearn their purpose.

I swallow the last of the wine in the mazer I'm holding and mutter something about the kitchen. Not one of them looks up. Owain's right about one thing—nobody would pay me any mind in the shadows, even if I went armed and inclined to cut a man good and proper.

The kitchen is cozy. Nest leans against the far wall, her eyes blank like coins. William is stacking scraps of wood with Not Miv, but when he sees me, he comes running. "Elen! Elen, can you get—him—to let me play outside? He says I'll get a thrashing if I do!"

No comfort, indeed. Keeping boys indoors would try a saint's patience. It's hard enough to convince Margred and the cousins to play knucklebones in the maidens' quarters when it's too wet for ball.

"I would if I could," I reply cheerfully, "but Owain ap Cadwgan is like a cat. He does what he wants."

William ventures a smile. "Does he play with his supper before killing it?"

I snort-laugh. From the mouths of babes. William is shuffling his feet and glancing longingly at the door, so very much like Margred that I pull up my hood, race across the courtyard to the king's chamber, and retrieve my ball from my rucksack. I'm back in moments, and I pitch it to him. "Since you can't play outside, play inside."

William tosses the ball from hand to hand, then bounces it off the wall and catches it. He's grinning like it's market day and he has a penny to spend. I'll have to make a new ball, but somehow I don't think Margred will mind.

David is curled in Nest's cloak under a table littered with scraps. When he sees me kneeling, he mutters *Alice* around the thumb in his mouth. I pull him out and into my lap, and I tell him a story that my mother used to tell Rhael and me when we were small, one about a girl from the sea who fell in love with a king whose hall stood high on a mountain.

When the story is finished, William sits down near his brother and rolls the ball to him. I slide out from under David, hoping he'll roll it back, but when he doesn't, William collects the ball and rolls it again. I edge close to Nest and wait for her to speak, but all she does is sway.

"Are you all right?" I finally ask.

"I don't think I can do this again," Nest says in a floaty, absent voice.

"The Normans took you away," I whisper.

She looks up, startled. Then she nods. "When I was a little girl. After my father was killed in battle. My older brother was smuggled away and took refuge abroad. My younger brother and I . . . weren't." Nest cuts her eyes toward me. "You were taken, too, weren't you? From a steading?"

Miv's cradle stood against the far wall. She was still crying when they shuffled Owain into a sling of canvas, him passed out, trailing blood, and gray as month-old oatmeal. Still crying when Einion put a hand between my shoulder blades and marched me toward the door, toward the square of bright blank daylight beyond. Ten steps and I could have grabbed her. But then they would have noticed her. Ten steps, but somewhere in the shadows, Rhael was making a sound like a lamb with a broken spine.

I should have thought of fire.

"I thought so," Nest breathes. "Oh saints, child."

Owain loves it when people speculate. He'd love Nest thinking that he dragged me screaming and crying to his bed. I can tell already she'd not believe me if I told her that he was in no condition to put a hand on me until well after I realized what I'd done and went willingly. Part of the playact was that Owain would keep me close, and even four-and-ten-year-old me had the sense to know what kind of close would serve me best.

Nest pulls me into a tight embrace. A comforting embrace. A mother's embrace.

I will not think of my mother. I don't pull away, though.

"Owain ap Cadwgan abducting my children and me to humiliate and taunt my husband is a horrible act of war," Nest whispers into my hair, "but holding a girl like you at his mercy is nothing but cruel for cruel's sake."

I saw it in his face as his color returned, as he got stronger, as the wound below his arm puckered and darkened. He had no more need of me. I'd brought him back from purgatory's doorstep, and now he'd turn me loose with a pat on the head and perhaps a coin in my hand, but without half a clue where I was or a house to go back to or any decent way to keep myself.

"I'm not here against my will." I edge gently out of her hug. "I'm Owain's protector. Saint Elen keeps him safe if he does the same for me."

Nest holds me at arm's length. "That's all? Oh, child. I'm sorry."

I bristle. "What for?"

"He didn't bring you here to be his wife or gain your parents' blessing to keep you at his hearth." She smiles sadly. "You may as well be a pet."

I will not remember my father, how he'd bind tiny dolls for us out of heather and slip them in our apron straps. I will not remember my mother or how she'd hum while she stirred the pottage or banked the fire. I will not remember how they kissed us each on the head and said they'd be back by nightfall, to keep the fire burning and add turnips to the pottage around midday so it would be ready upon their return.

"Owain keeps me close." I make a show of spinning Nest's bracelet around my wrist. "I am not a *pet*."

Nest slowly lifts a hand to cover her mouth. "Please don't tell me you think he loves you. I know you're young, but I don't think I can bear to hear that."

Owain loves his hunting dogs. He loves his warband. He most certainly loves the short sword he plundered off a dead Norman lord. Those are the things Owain ap Cadwgan loves.

But for three years now, Owain has put a roof over my head. I'm never hungry when he's not. He's bullied and beaten more than one man who's spoken roughly to me or out of turn. He has yet to raise a hand to me in anger.

"Or . . . saints, you're not going to tell me you love him, are you?"

There'll be no brothers two summers apart in steadings across a valley. Rhael will never be in my kitchen. No ballads at sundown, no giggling boy and girl swinging a leather bucket between them as they come up the path. Owain ap Cadwgan is the sole reason it'll never happen.

I snort quietly. Shake my head.

William has gotten David to return the ball to him by aiming it at his brother's forehead. The littler boy bats it back to keep from getting hit. William chortles, and David is almost smiling.

Then William tosses the ball to Nest and sings, "Now throw it to Elen, Mama, and she can throw it to David! David, sit on your backside and catch the ball, all right?"

David doesn't sit up, but he does pass his cloth square to his other hand and stretch out a palm.

Nest lets out a long breath and rubs her thumb over the tiny curve of sinew wrapped around the ball's opening. Then she unravels it with a flick of her fingernail and shows the flabby bladder to William. "In a moment, dear. Let's have Elen fix the ball first."

William nods and kneels to whisper to David.

As Nest hands me the bladder and sinew, she turns away from the boys and leans close. "This is probably a fool's errand, but you're out here with us instead of in there with him. So . . ." She takes a deep breath. "You must help me convince Owain ap Cadwgan to send my children back to their father. I cannot bear it, wondering what he might do to them on a whim. Not after what happened to my younger brother."

I turn all my attention to working the tiny piece of sinew into a loop around the pucker in the bladder. She couldn't have forgotten that's why they're here at all.

"I know it can't be me. Going back to Gerald. I'm not asking that. But help *them*. Please. I'll make it worth your while."

Her servant's linsey is stained. Her feet are wrapped in rags. Her hair is tied back with the kind of hemp twine that binds undressed fleeces. Yet Nest stands chin up, shieldlike, as if there's a clatter in the yard outside.

"Please." Her voice breaks. "There must be something you want."

My steading unburned. My parents bustling around hearth and yard and byre. Brothers two summers apart, Rhael at my door. Miv as big as Margred, playing hoodman-blind with my son and daughter.

I cinch the sinew tight.

"Elen?" William has pulled David upright, balancing the

littler boy and helping him hold his palms outstretched to catch the ball. "Look, we're ready!"

"There is," I say quietly to Nest, and I toss the ball to the boys, pick up the mazer that one of the kitchen lads refilled, and squish through the rain toward the hall.

Owain is very drunk when I pad back inside. Good. He's a suggestible and happy drunk. I slide behind him and begin rubbing his shoulders. His muscles are knotted up like bad beef, and he grunts appreciation.

"My lord?"

"Yes, sweeting?" His voice is a low rumble, like a purring cat.

"Is it true you won't let the little ones play outside?"

Owain tries to swivel to look at me, but I knead harder and he stills.

"I heard them raising a clamor when I was coming back from the privy," I add.

"No comfort. If you don't like hearing them squawk, stay away from them."

I lean close and whisper in his ear, "Makes me wonder what Gerald of Windsor would do, hearing this story out of turn."

"Out of turn how?" Owain's voice is mellow, easy as honey. He's humoring me.

"Right now, all Gerald has are his own worst thoughts." I push my thumbs along Owain's shoulder bones, roll them up the muscles. "What if those thoughts went even darker? A few stories from his frightened children — the little ones he left to

you when he fled down the privy shaft to save his own neck—
well, a murderous father has even less wits than a murderous
husband, wouldn't you think?"

"What are you saying?"

The bench shudders, and Einion penteulu drops next to
Owain. "She's telling you to return the brats to Gerald. Just like
your *father* told you."

Owain's back turns to stone beneath my hands. Einion
calmly reaches for a mug of wine. The silence grows uncomfortable. I can't keep talking, though. Not in front of Einion
penteulu. Because he's right.

"Oh, don't stop on my account." Einion's face is hidden by
the mug, but I can hear the smirk in his voice. "Saint Elen was
doing what she does best."

"Have some more wine." I bare a gritty smile, snatch his
mug out of his hand, and pour.

"Is that what you're doing?" Owain asks me. "Because I told
you. No comfort."

"I was . . ." I was about to tell him how bad it is not knowing,
but how it's a different kind of bad when you have pieces that
make you *think* you know. Gerald would have William and his
teary, wide-eyed tales of barefoot marches and his mother with
soup burns over her wrists, crossing the courtyard head down
behind Owain. He'd have David's staring silence, his muttered
Alice. He'd have Not Miv, who'd cry and cry.

"She was whispering in your ear," Einion penteulu fills in
helpfully, "and rubbing your shoulders."

"And telling me to let them go," Owain says, like he's putting pieces together in his head.

I pull my hands away from Owain's back. "No. No, my lord. Not *let* them go."

"But?" prompts Einion, drawing the word out, tipping his mug at me.

That mug would make a nice deep dent in the side of Einion penteulu's wretched head.

"I don't think I understand," Einion goes on in a mocking halfwit drawl. "I'm but a simple fighting man. Perhaps you should come over here and explain it in pretty whispers while rubbing my shoulders."

Owain slams his mug down, but Einion penteulu is already sliding away on the bench with both hands up as if in surrender.

"Beg pardon, my lord." Einion bows his head. "That was out of turn."

Owain slides an arm around my waist and pulls me against him without taking his eyes off Einion penteulu. "Yes. It was."

I can't help but slice a grin at Einion, but it doesn't matter, for he's standing to like any of the lads in the practice yard, gaze blanked, squared up.

After several long moments, Owain bids me pour more wine and asks if I might rub his shoulders a little longer. His voice is easy once again, and Einion penteulu retakes his seat, and before long they're laughing at a wolfhound licking its nether parts. When their conversation devolves into whether it's too cold for a pissing contest, I move my hands away and drift kitchenward, but I'm not two steps from the trestle when Owain pretends to collapse on the bench.

"Thief!" He lolls across the table, flopping his wrists like fish on a riverbank. "Take away my muscles and bones, will you? Put 'em back, sweeting, or I'm of no use to anyone."

Then Owain tips his head enough to grin at me. Einion penteulu snickers and takes another drink. I sigh and start rubbing Owain's shoulders again. I also keep pouring the wine, but he's no fool. I can't even glance at the hall door without him going limp like David and moaning about bone theft and floggings.

When Owain says no comfort, he does not act in half measures.

March 1110

I BLINK AWAKE WHEN OWAIN SHIFTS QUICK AND
sudden, and I scrabble hard when Einion penteulu's face appears
above the bed.

"He's on us," Einion says grimly. "Get up. Arm yourself."

Owain squints at him, the bedclothes tumbling to his waist.
"Who?"

"Your whoreson cousin Madog, rot his soul! Bought and
paid for by Gerald of Windsor and that bastard English king!"

"Goddamn it!" Owain rolls out of bed, cursing as he puts on
his tunic — *dawn raid that son of a* — but my hands are trembling
as I slide into my gown and grab my rucksack. Madog ap Rhirid
who thought to be Owain's penteulu. Who Owain humiliated in
the public of his father's hall and again in the yard in front of all
the warbands. Whose sister is a child of eleven and the only one
of Owain's entire volatile family who looks forward to seeing me.

Gerald did not come hellbent. Nor did he come with a big Norman army. He chose more thorough means.

The hall is in chaos. The lads are stumbling over one another, grappling with weapons and cursing whorebegotten Madog ap Rhirid and all his kin to eight generations. In the corner, at Nest's feet, William is trying to fasten his hose and keeps fumbling the ties. I start toward him, but Owain pulls me up short.

"You're with me," he says. "Einion will see to Nest and Gerald's brats."

I struggle, but Owain's grip tightens. "There won't be a fight. This is an ambush. We're getting the hell out of here."

"Alice! Alice! *Alice!*" David thrashes in Nest's arms, red-faced, small hands grabbing, but Owain tows me stumbling toward the door.

Outside, the sky is a harsh screaming pink, and it's bone-chill freezing. Armed men are flooding around both corners of the hall and through the trees, and I paw the air to my left and panic when Rhael isn't there gripping and regripping the butcher knife. There's nothing in my hand, when only a moment ago she shoved the fire iron at me and told me not to be afraid. Miv is not crying oh Christ they got to her already Rhael said they would not care about—

—a heavy weight falls on my arm and I jerk into unsteady motion and something catches my sleeve but it's Owain pulling me along I recognize his coppery curls it's not—

—Llywelyn penteulu who moves toward me in the steading's dim light slow like a snake I clutch the fire iron it slips in my sweaty hand a man who looks like him hulks forward too fast grabs me by the wrist and I bring down the fire iron and there's—

—blood everywhere men shouting fleeing headlong Owain ahead of me blood down one arm—

—there on the floor of the steading with Rhael's knife buried to the hilt under his arm he looks dead already but I said I could save him and that's why Einion ap Tewdwr made them let me up and I kneel beside him aching and shaken and bellysick skin crawling Christ now what do I do—

—I follow that's what I do because they burned my house they burned everything in the vale and they killed them both and seized all the beasts and now I follow because there is nothing else and there is nothing else because of Owain ap Cadwgan who I follow—

†

It's long past full dark when Owain stops moving. My wrist hurts from where he kept hold of me, and there's a blurry bloodsmear where his grip was. Owain stops moving because he collapses against a tree and slides down the trunk till he's slumped among the roots. He's muttering something, and I hear my name.

The dawn raid scattered the warband, and the greenwood is empty but for us. I'm crouching into a hedge. I'm cold. I should say something. Go to him. This morning I was safe in a hunting lodge. Now I'm in the wilderness. Madog ap Rhirid swept down with fire and sword and would have kicked in the door were it not for Owain ap Cadwgan.

Then I realize Owain is thanking Saint Elen for keeping him. I lay my cheek on my knees.

There's a measure of forest stillness, then Owain draws a long breath, lets it out in a whistle, and smiles at me halfway. "Well then. That was much closer than I like. You keep pace like a warbander. Like you were born in the field."

There was no clatter in the dooryard. Madog came swift and silent and single-minded, his own vengeance at hand as much as Gerald's, and I have Einion ap Tewdwr to thank once more for helping to pull me clear.

"Sweeting? You're not hurt, are you? Come here."

He beckons and I cannot go. He's the one who grabbed Rhael. He's the one who came to my vale to burn, to unman whatever lord held the ground beneath my steading. He beckons me to the curtained bed when the scar beneath his arm is finally healed. Saint Elen turns her back because this is what I asked her for. I begged for my life and she granted it.

I stumble over to him. Just as I did then. I let him put an arm around me. Just as I did then. I curl against him because he's warm. Because he's always kept me safe and close to him. Because I made him this way with effort, with will, with intent. As the months became years, I held my breath a little less with each raid.

What Owain did to Gerald of Windsor was not a raid, though. The moment Nest put one bloodied bare foot into the courtyard, the war Cadwgan planned became something else entirely.

Something my playact was never intended to cope with.

Owain says we should start moving once more, but I can't take more than three steps before my muscles turn to water and I sink. So he sets trip lines, then gathers me under his arm and pulls his cloak over us both. I lay my head on his shoulder and close my eyes so I don't have to see darkness seeping through bony winter trees in and down and toward us.

He's talking. His voice murmurs like a stream over rocks and rumbles against my ear. *Something something* northward *something something* Gerald of Windsor. Low and calm and confident. Even now. The voice of a man with a saint over his shoulder, unquestioning.

When Owain shifts into *something something* Nest *something something* Einion penteulu, I can't bring myself to listen any longer because he might be talking about William and David and Not Miv, how Einion was to *look to them,* how Einion will not hesitate to kill the children and their mother if it means keeping Madog from recapturing them and returning them to Gerald of Windsor.

I can't tell Owain that Saint Elen said Gerald has more than paid whatever blood debt he owes to Owain's warband. That every man the length and breadth of the kingdoms of Wales and the border too has received his message grim and clear. I can't tell him that Nest asked me what I wanted like she would give it to me.

Saint Elen would likely say all these things and more, but I will not say them for her. I dare not. She is the saint, not me. So I stay silent. I wrap my arms tight around him, but not before I run my thumb over the place where armor hides his scar.

EVERY FORT WE SIGHT OR PASS WHERE WE MIGHT
take refuge is a burned-out husk. We find the charred timbers of
what used to be steadings, and the holy houses are clearly being
watched with an eye to ambush. Owain moves a little quicker.
His temper gets shorter. He curses his cousin again and again as
if this is Madog's fault alone. Neither of us sleeps.

Then we come across a fort that's untouched but already
half-abandoned. As people stream out, hauling whatever they
can carry, the steward meets us in the courtyard and tells
Owain that none of Cadwgan's allies have so much as lifted
a finger against Madog's warband, and Owain's mouth falls
open.

"*None* of them? They're our kinsmen! They've sworn their
swords to us!"

The steward nods sadly. "You should be grateful none are leading a warband against you. Madog ap Rhirid has had no trouble finding men to join him who have an ax to grind."

"Son of a bastard . . ."

"The English king is making it very worth their while, too," the steward says. "He's promised Powys to whoever can take it from your father, be he Welsh or Norman."

Owain grunts. "Like it's his to promise."

"And"—the steward squints at the horizon—"Gerald of Windsor has put a price on your head. The word is Madog ap Rhirid is going around saying it's as good as spent."

"How much?"

"Ten silver pennies to the man who brings him your head. Fifty for you still alive."

Owain mimics frigging off and cackles insolently. I turn my eyes Heavenward even as I want to slap him hard, because that kind of carrot's going to drive a lot of donkeys.

"God Almighty, I hope he gets close enough to try." Owain glances around the emptying courtyard. "Any of my warband here?"

The steward shakes his head. "Fighting men are gathering at the fort by the river. Where your lord father is, and where you ought to go right away."

Owain surveys the sky, frowning. He holds nothing that's his alone. Powys and everything in it belongs to his father. The province of Ceredigion, too. Most of the time he's welcome at every fort in the kingdom, but right now, turning up anywhere but where Cadwgan is will have the look of treason. Like he's joining Madog and the English king.

"Your cousin and his lot are only two valleys down. Stay here and you face him alone." The steward shoulders a rucksack and pulls a burning stave out of a massive bonfire raging in the center of the yard. "Give me a hand?"

Two valleys down. I crane my neck for curls of black smoke rising between low-slung hills, and sure enough, they're clawing their way skyward, and this time I know them for what they are. Owain marks them, too. He mutters something vulgar, then nods. He and the steward take up firebrands and run them along the edges of lean-tos and piles of straw. They toss them into stables and into the hall. Other men join them, and soon the whole fort is ablaze.

I move outside the gate and pull up my hood. Nothing will remain for Madog to seize or plunder, but there'll also not be a hot meal or anything resembling a bed. Owain appears out of the smoke, coughing into his sleeve, followed by the steward and the last few men from the fort. Once outside, they scatter in different directions, bound for the hills to stand over their families as Madog's warband moves in.

Everything is not in hand. If it were, we'd be at Llyssun. Cozy fire. A half-decent privy. Margred would be there, too, making up stories about her toy mouse. Owain and Einion penteulu would be pleasantly drunk and playing flinches, flicking lit twigs at each other and punching whoever moves. The lads would be feeding the wolfhounds cheese to make them fart, wagering on which dog's wind will be the loudest. Rhys would be lifting his bucket and touching that scar.

I keep pace with Owain as we head northward. Even when the fort's burning shell is out of sight, I can still smell smoke.

"Fouled up. All of it."

Owain speaks to his feet caked with mud and bare legs covered with scratches, to the ground sliding beneath him at a pace I struggle to match. It's just him and me. No one to parade around full of bravado. His voice is quiet now, like we're in some church nave that begs for a measure of stillness.

"I thought Gerald of Windsor would come himself. Steel flashing. Warhorses snorting. I was bloody well *counting* on it. But why under Christ the English king has made it his concern . . ."

I almost remind Owain how badly that king wants a Norman lord holding Cadwgan's realm, but that will only remind him of his father, and I've no wish to interrupt what might be the closest thing to an apology Owain ap Cadwgan is likely to make.

"Nest is important to him?" I offer instead, and I slant it like a question so Owain will not bristle overmuch.

He does, a little, but then he sighs. "Mayhap. It must be years since the English king even saw her, though. It's been an age since their son was sent out to fosterage and she was wed to Gerald of Windsor. It makes no sense! Gerald's difficulties should have barely made the king look up from his breakfast."

To Owain ap Cadwgan, this has only ever had to do with Gerald of Windsor. To Henry, king of the English, it also has to do with Nest. And Cadwgan's kingdom.

Cadwgan's fealty as well.

"I just . . ." Owain looks away. "I had it all worked out. It was going to be better than any war my father planned. It was going to gut Dyfed of its strongest defender and lay it bare to invasion. We could have seized whole districts. Mayhap the entire province! That, sweeting, should have been my final vengeance on Gerald of bloody Windsor. After having to imagine what sport I was making of his wife and what harm I might visit on his children, that he would live long enough to know that his ill-gotten lands were now occupied by the house of Bleddyn, before I wiped God's green earth clean of him."

I nod. I slip my hand in his.

"Times like this," Owain says quietly, "I wish I had a saint's counsel as well as her protection."

Times like this I'm glad he doesn't. Times like this I thank every saint that my playact has no such promise. It's hard enough to keep from saying aloud what both of us are thinking.

"Now . . . God rot it, I'll have to go to him. The smug bastard." Owain twists up his face and mimics his father: "I've been killing Normans longer than you've been alive. Shut up and go plunder something."

I can't help but smirk, but there's truth to it. Those long-ago victories against the Normans happened across Wales when I was still in my cradle, and all of them at the hand of Cadwgan ap Bleddyn. If anyone can help Owain bring Gerald of Windsor and the English king to a standstill—by charm, by parley, by the sword—it's Cadwgan.

And he'll be in a position to dictate a price.

WE ARRIVE AT THE RIVER FORT IN THE LATE AFTER-
noon. Many of the lads have regrouped here, milling restlessly
in the muddy yard or sharpening weapons or playing flinches.
Rhys is near the gate, and he's the first to extend a shy wrist to
Owain, who clasps it and mocks a blow to Rhys's neck. Both of
them grin. As Owain moves toward his warband, Rhys nods to
me, solemn, before shaking his hair over his eyes and following
his lord. Owain soon disappears among the lads, slapping backs
and mussing hair. He does not seem to notice his father standing
on the wall walk with his hands behind his back, regarding the
countryside beyond.

There's no way Cadwgan didn't see us arrive. No way this
isn't going to be bad. I brace for the storming down, the raging, the strong possibility of knuckles flying, but Cadwgan ap
Bleddyn does not move.

A small hooded head appears in the kitchen doorway, then William comes squealing across the mud and throws himself against me and holds on hard. "Elen! Elen, you're all right!"

For the longest moment I just hold the boy around his knobby shoulders with his golden hair flossy against my cheek. I left him to burn but he did not burn, and now I never want to let him go.

William squirms out of my hug and takes my hand. "Come see David. He won't eat. Mama's having fits over it."

"He's not hurt, is he?"

William considers. "I don't think so. He just lies where you put him. Sometimes he'll whisper *Alice*. That's why I think you can fix him. He was better when you were around."

"Better?" Clinging to my shoulder and sucking his thumb and worrying his little rag does not sound like *better*.

"Much," William replies without hesitation. "I thought my brother would never talk again after . . . you know. When they took us away. One of them shouted at David to shut up because he was crying. So he shut up."

Nest is in the hearth corner, David across her lap doing that staring slow blink. At her side, Not Miv piles scraps of wood and bats them over. All of them are grubby, and Nest's cheeks are hollow, but none of them look harmed in a way fleeing a vengeful army wouldn't cause.

Einion penteulu looked to them. Pulled them clear.

"Then there was you," William rattles on, towing me toward his family like a small, determined cart horse, "and you picked him up just like Alice used to. You told stories, too." With his free hand, William shifts his cloak enough to show my ball dangling from a length of twine tied around his waist. "I hid it from him. The warbander that brought us here. If I kept it safe, I knew you'd come back. And you did!"

None of them burned. I blink away tears and squeeze William's hand. "Good lad."

"Now that you're back, David will be better. We can play ball again. You, me, David, and Mama. Angharad can watch. She'd just chew on the ball if we let her play."

I'd hug William hard if Nest weren't here. Instead I clap his back warband-style, then kneel and pet David's hair. It's dark like Miv's was, smooth and silky.

"Hey, duckling," I say to him cheerfully, like I'd just stepped out to use the privy. "Are you hungry? I wager you're hungry. Would you like some oatcakes and honey?"

David turns at the sound of my voice and says, "Alice." He rolls over in his mother's arms and reaches for me. Nest lets him go, then tries to hide wiping her eyes. David clings to my shoulder, and I sway toward the trestle board with William tagging puppylike at my elbow. The honey isn't on the table or any of the shelves, so I ask the cook where it is.

"There's but a whisper left, pet," he says, "and it's not for you."

I draw back, stung. David on my shoulder snuffles. William sighs like he's heard this before.

"I don't want it for me." I hoist David higher. "It's for them."

"Not for them, either. Gonna glaze the last of the venison."

"Honey," whispers David. "Honey Alice please."

I settle David on a bench next to William, then square up like a bull. "Use blackcurrant. It makes a better glaze anyway. Or perhaps you'd like to explain to Owain ap Cadwgan, who's just arrived from a se'ennight in the field, why I can't have that honey."

The cook looks uneasy, but he fetches the pot off some hidden shelf. I scrape the insides bare and slather a gooey pile of honey on two thick oatcakes. David presses his shoulder against his brother's and does not take his eyes from the door. I want to tell them both not to be afraid, but instead I stand over them while they eat every crumb and lick their fingers twice.

I KNOW IT'S GOING TO BE BAD. IT'S SUPPER BEFORE I find out how bad.

Cadwgan ap Bleddyn appears in the hall doorway with Nest on his arm, polite and formal, like she's his daughter. She's wearing a proper gown, but it's too big through the shoulders and she's rolled the cuffs over her wrists. Her plaits are sagging like pitiful cow pats, like she fixed them herself, and she's cringing away from Cadwgan the smallest bit as she stares hard at the floor.

Owain is sitting in the king's chair at the high table, but as soon as his father appears, he shifts to the heir apparent's place in a slow, offhand way, like he was just keeping the seat warm. Cadwgan takes his rightful position and puts Nest at his left. He runs a slow, disdainful look over Owain, then turns to me and says, "Pour." Or rather, he says it to the wall behind my head.

I pour wine for men all the time, but precious few will speak to me like that. Not twice, anyway. Owain's eyes narrow, but before he can do something foolhardy, I pick up the flagon and move toward the table. At least one of us must keep this from going from bad to worse.

"Well, Da," Owain says lightly into the stiff silence, "you said you wanted a war."

"Not with my nephew," Cadwgan growls, "and definitely not with any of my onetime allies. To say nothing for the English king! But no. You had to have your precious vengeance."

"I brought you leverage"—Owain's color is rising—"against the very bastard whoreson we all know must fall if what's ours is to stay ours."

Cadwgan's face goes hard. "Leverage? Merciful Christ, you brought me a *liability*! Now Gerald gets to go to his good friend, the English king, and play the wronged party all rumpled and sorrowful. No one is looking too hard anymore at who he sends his warband against and whose birthright he's got his eye on. That's your doing, son. Now men see only your one act, not all of his."

"Da—"

"Now you've come to me," Cadwgan goes on, slow, drawling, "to pull your bacon out of the fire. Me, who's been crossing steel with Normans since before you were born. Who expanded his kingdom and held it against the English king's efforts to put Norman lords in every district when you were still playing with toy swords."

Owain looks ready to throw knuckles or sob, and either would be disastrous. Nest is fighting a smile.

"I'll go to the English king's representatives on your behalf," Cadwgan tells Owain, "and see what terms I can manage for this dog's breakfast. Nest and the children *will* go back to Gerald and you *will* take ship immediately for Waterford."

My hand jerks. Hard. Take ship for *what*?

"I am not fleeing to Ireland like a frightened child," Owain snaps.

Cadwgan collars Owain across the shoulders rough but fond, like he might a warbander. "Lad, this is the way it's done. There's no shame in it. Hell, I did it myself once upon a time."

"Take your hand off me, Da," Owain says, low and ominous.

I can't tell Owain that Saint Elen said to shut his big foolish mouth and take his medicine. That if this is Cadwgan ap Bleddyn's price, Owain is getting a bargain by half.

Cadwgan leaves his arm around Owain's shoulder for a very long moment so the hall can see him do it, then he pulls away and turns to Nest. "I'll have men I trust personally escort you and your children homeward, my lady. You'll leave at first light on the morrow. I . . . realize it's probably meaningless, but I'd have you know this was never meant to happen."

Nest snorts quietly, then at length looks Cadwgan in the eye and says, "Thank you."

"And *you*." Cadwgan aims his meat knife at Owain. "You will sail to Ireland in the first ship that'll take you. You will find the king of Munster — no, he's the high king now — and with my compliments you will give him that dagger with the ruby in the hilt and that silver bird-head cloak pin. Muirchertach Ua Briain is an ally and a friend, and you will not cause him a single moment of grief. You will also not put one foot anywhere in Wales until I bid you. Clear?"

Owain nods. He's glaring pure murder at his folded hands.

Ireland. A whole sea between us and the many warbands converging on Owain ap Cadwgan. No one to claim the price on his head. A nice long exile for people to forget Nest was ever dragged barefoot from her bed and kept in hearth corners covered in soot, her children snuffling and cold around her.

Most people, at least. Gerald of Windsor will never forget, much like Owain will not forget what was done to Llywelyn penteulu. Neither will let it lie until one of them is dead. Mayhap not even then.

Cadwgan will see Nest and the little ones safely back to Gerald of Windsor, though. He'll do it in a way that looks generous. Magnanimous, even.

The little ones will be safe. William with his long silly stories and jokes that don't make sense, his endlessly bouncing my ball on one knee just like Margred when she has to wait for anything. David and his square of rag, how much he loves my mother's old stories. Not Miv, her sweet milk smell, her wispy Miv-dark hair, how she perches on my arm without holding on like it's unthinkable I might let her fall.

They will be home with their mother and father and all the

beasts in the byre. They will be a family again, just like the clatter in their dooryard never was.

Cadwgan curtly bids me gone partway through the meal and gives Owain a look that begs him to backtalk, but Owain wisely grits a smile and nods me toward the door. I head straight to the kitchen. If I'm to say farewell properly, it has to be now. There's to be no comfort, and on the morrow something is sure to keep me from orderly cloak-tying and tucking packets of travel bread into wool-wrapped hands and giving kisses on round red cheeks.

I have a pretty good idea that something will involve warm breath on my neck and a lazy hand drifting up my belly.

I find the children under one of the trestles. They're playing a game William calls border raids. He's holding Not Miv around the middle so she can't crawl away or eat rubbish off the floor.

"She's my horse," William explains.

"My horse," David says, holding up his ratty cloth.

I join them under the table and ask who they're raiding, how many spoils they've carried away, what they've burned. William spins out a story about a ford and an ambush and five thousand Norman knights. David slides against me and grips my hand, damp and sticky.

They'll be out of danger. Untangled from the war Owain tried to "enhance" and free from his attempt at vengeance that they never should have been part of in the first place. They'll be out of danger, and I'll never see them again on this earth.

William holds his giggling sister's smock like reins, tugging her left and right, while David sucks his thumb and waves his rag like a banner. The older boy talks faster, and now there are a hundred thousand knights and the ford runs red with blood and they have so much plunder that he needs David to bear some of it on his horse, so David slides away from me toward his brother, squealing, "I carry it! Me, I carry!"

Feet clomp past. Einion penteulu. There aren't many reasons he'd come into the kitchen, and none of them are good. Cadwgan has released Nest and the little ones, and it must be that Owain will not let such a thing stand.

Einion penteulu must be here to kill them.

I put a finger to my lips and William pauses mid-sword-stab, head cocked. "It's the enemy," I breathe into his ear. "We must be quiet so we'll not give away our position."

William nods, grinning, and puts his own finger to his lips at David. David looks between me and his brother, eyes huge. I give him my miracle-girl smile. *Absolutely nothing is amiss, this is all a game, and the enemy will never find us.* David does not scramble back against me. He's wary, but he stays near William and holds tight to his rag.

Einion penteulu stomps toward the rear of the kitchen, asks the cook something, swears, and heads outside once more. I wait till the echo of footfalls is gone some moments, then let out a long breath and turn to the little ones. They must keep out of sight till I can put a stop to this.

"You stay here and guard this border," I whisper. "William, you're the king. David, you're penteulu. Don't let the enemy past, and don't let them take your livestock." I pet Not Miv's soft hair. "Stay together, and don't leave your position."

"Not go," David says, and he grapples the end of my cloak into the same fist as his cloth scrap.

I shush him and glance at the door. Einion penteulu will be back when he can't find them anywhere else. "I'll be a scout. I'll go find where the enemy is hiding. I'll make sure he thinks we're somewhere else."

"Not *go*," David repeats, doubling my cloak-end in his grip.

"Stand to, field captain," William says cheerfully to him. "She'll be back. She came to find us after we had to leave with that warbander all in a rush. Right, scout?"

David draws a sobby breath and wrings my cloak-end. If I pull away and leave, he'll cry. If he cries, Einion penteulu will be back in a heartbeat, blade in hand. So I nod. Instead of saying farewell, like I came here to do. Then, because his eyes are so big and swimming, I tell him, "Duckling, I'll always come back."

"Told you," William says to David as he gentles my cloak out of his brother's fist. "You've your orders, scout. My field captain and I will ambush the next warband that happens past."

"A good ambush needs *quiet*," I remind them. "Hold your border here and stay together."

I slide out from under the table. David makes a tiny puppy sound even as William whispers something in his ear and firmly closes his brother's fingers around the red cloth square like it's a fire iron.

———+———

I'll find Owain. I'll convince him. I'll beg. I'll promise him anything. He said no comfort, but that's a world away from murder in cold blood.

I'll go to Cadwgan if need be.

The yard is mostly empty, growing dark and freezing besides, and I'm halfway across when Rhys falls into step beside me, hooded and dressed for weather. He gestures to a handful of horses standing saddled near the well. Owain appears at the stable door with a groom. They speak briefly, and Owain passes him something round and silver while glancing over his shoulder at the hall.

"Hurry," mutters Rhys, and he nudges me forward with the arm I healed.

I do as I'm told. Madog and his warband must be closer than anyone thought for us to take horse right now when we should be looking toward supper and bed. Cadwgan will be scrambling too, to set Nest up with an escort home. It'll go hard for him if he's not the one to give her and the little ones back to Gerald.

The little ones I just lied to. I'll not be coming back. Not ever. I could have said farewell. Given them each one last hug.

Owain grins when he sees me and plants a kiss on my forehead. He holds out my rucksack, and I shoulder it as Einion penteulu appears like a ghost, holding the elbow of a cloaked figure I can tell at a glance is Nest just by the way she carries herself.

Surely Cadwgan is not fool enough to bid Owain return Nest and the little ones to Gerald. Even were that so, the children are still in the kitchen and not ready to travel. The rest of the lads are nowhere in sight, and Owain would ride in full force on such an errand. The horses are Cadwgan's, though. I'd know that bridle tooling anywhere.

"Right then." Owain steadies the stirrup of a bay mare and smiles at Nest, cold and dangerous. "Up you go."

"Where are my children?" she asks.

Einion cuts his eyes to Owain and makes the warband field gesture for *deception* behind Nest's back. Nest looks from me to Owain, then she buries an elbow in Einion penteulu's ribs and tries to break away, but Einion has two handfuls of her cloak and she's pulled up hard, choking, gasping. Owain seizes her wrist and waist, pinning her against him while Rhys draws steel and blocks the view from the hall with his turned back.

"Listen closely," Owain growls in her ear, "and don't you dare make a sound. Your brats will be fine. My father will see them returned to your whoreson coward husband, but you are coming with us to Ireland, and I swear before God Almighty and all the saints that I am prepared to make your captivity up to this point seem like paradise should you decide to make trouble."

I cannot look at Nest. I should have known. I should have at least suspected.

Nest's indrawn breaths are loud and shaky. At length she nods. A small motion. Small and helpless.

"Now get on that horse," Owain says, "and be quick about it."

Nest hoists herself into the saddle all in shudders like a

puppet on strings. She takes the reins, and they slide limp like ribbons through her fingers. She doesn't even flinch when Einion penteulu pulls her hood sharp across her face.

"We're leaving here easy and slow," Owain goes on, pulling his own horse about. "No notice. No alarm. No *trouble*."

We do. We ride one after another through the yard, out the gate, and into the frigid twilight, and no one pays us any mind. We ride later than we should, till Owain is smacked in the face by low branches once too often and bids us halt and scratch out a camp. While Owain and Einion penteulu whisper-argue about security and visibility and Rhys stands by resigned, waiting to get the worst watch, I guide Nest into a stand of brush and push a field wineskin into her hands. She holds it but doesn't drink.

"It's not how you meant it to happen," I tell her, "but the little ones are away from Owain. Cadwgan has every reason to return them to their father now, and he'll move Heaven and earth to do it."

"My babies," she whispers. "They'll be so frightened. All alone."

"You'll be back with them before you know it," I say, but Nest merely lowers her head onto her knees, the wineskin dangling from her fingers.

They are safe. They're together. They're going home.

I take the wineskin from Nest and drink deep. Even though I did not leave them to save my own skin, even though I left them to save theirs, to them it will only matter that I didn't come back.

April 1110

I've seen ships at wharf and ships under sail, but I have never been close enough to mark the green sludge crusting the waterline, the splintery, graying wood, the low and ominous creaks leaking from somewhere within like an old man's windy guts.

"A pity Saint Elen will not tell Owain he'll die at sea," mutters Einion penteulu, and for once I agree with him even as I wish he'd keep his mouth shut.

"Say that a little louder," I reply under my breath. "Owain's *quite* in the humor to hear it."

We both study Owain, standing on the wharf-end with his back to us watching a rowboat approach. He's long since traded his leather armor for a night's lodging and now wears a drover's coarseweave tunic, but I'd wager real drovers don't constantly complain of the itching. In addition to Gerald's bounty, the

English king has put a price of ten shillings on Owain's head. Owain brags it should be twenty, but he always sits facing the door and hasn't been cold sober since we arrived in this little harbor town.

Einion penteulu nods toward Nest where she slumps, washrag-limp, against a nearby post. "You mind your tasks. I'll mind mine."

I should be grateful Nest isn't plotting ways to steal a dagger and stab Owain repeatedly in the vitals, but I know the look about her all too well. It comes on you when Einion ap Tewdwr whispers grim in your ear that they killed them both and seized all the beasts, and in that moment you realize that you will never again have a home unless you make one yourself by hook and by crook, by warp and by weft.

The rowboat pulls up to the wharf, and the sailor at the oars nods to Owain. The boat seems small and manageable, but I can't look away from the dark water beneath. I can't swim. Neither can Owain. Einion penteulu and Rhys climb into the boat, but Nest hesitates, clinging to the brine-damp post.

"Be quick about it," Owain grumbles.

"Be easy!" I snap. "You could have let her go home with her children. You didn't have to drag her along with us."

"What, I was just going to give her back? Like my father wanted?" Owain makes a flighty gesture and simpers, "Oh, here you are, Gerald of bloody Windsor who killed my penteulu in cold blood, please take your beautiful wife back. I'll just admit defeat now and go cower in Ireland under another man's sword-arm." His voice goes hard again. "Sorry, sweeting, but I hope to Christ you know that's never going to happen."

Nest closes her eyes.

The rowboat sways under us as the sailor works the oars. Soon we're alongside the merchant cog, and a rope ladder tumbles down till it dangles above the rowboat's flank. The sailor at the oars nods us toward it while he keeps the boat close to the ship in the choppy water. Rhys climbs first, rung by agonizing rung as the cog dips and groans in the swells, until he disappears over the side. Then Einion penteulu nudges me. I put on my miracle face and climb. When I reach the top, a sailor helps me over the side of the ship with one meaty hand on my forearm and the other on my backside. He says something to his fellows that's a slurry of liquid sounds, but it makes them cackle like jackdaws.

This has the look of a teulu at sea, and we are far from anywhere Owain might have sway.

I make a show of putting myself near Rhys even though he clutches the ship rail and looks the worst kind of greensick. Rhys is coltish, but he towers over many men by at least a handswidth, and when he shifts closer to me and touches his forearm, the sailors go back to their rope hauling and crate stacking even as they size him up sidelong.

Einion penteulu appears at the top of the ladder, then Nest, and finally Owain. A sailor directs us with stabs of his finger to the back of the ship, so I get a good view of the sailors busying themselves with ropes and canvas and oars, calling to one another in that strange tongue I can't follow. Nest curls up beside a crate while Einion joins Rhys and Owain at the rail.

I hang back. I want to know how long the crossing will be, how Owain will know where to find the high king, what we'll do if Cadwgan's old brother in arms has no welcome for us. But after we traded the horses Owain "obtained" from his father to pay our passage, Einion penteulu tried asking how long we'd be away, and Owain told him to shut his gob or draw his blade.

So now we all leave Owain be and let him growl about what a bastard his father is, how ill his cousin Madog ap Rhirid served him, how the English king and Gerald of Windsor could do very improbable things to each other. It's safer that way, even though betimes it's hard not to remind Owain that he'd be raiding and plundering quite merrily had he not abducted the wife of the lord of Dyfed for pure vengeance, or had he given her back when offered the chance.

THE SEA IS GRAY AND JAGGEDY. IT'S LOVELY IN THE way of bleak things. The sails rattle overhead, and the wind tugs at my cloak. Everything smells so clean and wind-raked, nothing like the stale harbor behind us or the worrisome damp of brackish wood beneath.

Owain, Rhys, and Einion penteulu spend most of their time at the rail studying the water as if they know a damn thing about it. Nest stays folded in a hollow between two crates of something pungent. Her hood falls heavy over her forehead and her body curls itself into shadows. All I can see of her is a slant of pale cheek slashed by a loose strand of hair.

The day passes slow, but when it's getting toward evening, I put together some cheese and meat for us all from our rucksack of stale provisions. Owain, Rhys, and Einion penteulu take theirs with muttered thanks. I've saved the best portion, even though I don't expect Nest to eat it. I kneel at her side and touch her shoulder. Her hood shudders and there's a muffled sob. I slip the food in my apron, edge myself into the hollow beside her, and draw her close like she's one of the children. Nest sobs again, chokes, presses both hands against her eyes.

"Damn him," she mutters. "This was the one thing. I wasn't going to give him this, too."

"You're not. Owain's clear over there. I won't tell." I squeeze her shoulders in a way I mean to be playful and reassuring, but Nest goes still and tense under my arm.

"I should . . . thank you. While I can. For everything you've done for my children. I was . . . not at my best. You just *did* for them. Now they love you."

I told them I'd be back. William must worry that the enemy got me. Not Miv will peek under blankets like a game of where-is-baby. David may never be better again.

"There's just one thing I need to know." Nest picks at her fraying sleeve. "Did you really enjoy their company? Or were you just doing as he told you?"

I stiffen. "Saints, that you can even ask me that."

"That first day. When we . . . arrived. The look on your face."

Little hands. That milk smell. I couldn't. But Owain turned away like there was no chance I'd do anything else. Left them to me so he could sort out the rest of the plunder. The little *weh-weh-weh* was a tiny sound in the chaos of the courtyard and yet louder than anything else. Nest cringing whenever he spoke, wrung out like a rag but with her baby safe against her heart and not left in a cradle in some corner to burn.

"I didn't want to love them," I reply to my hands, "but I do."

Nest leans close. "Who's Miv?"

I choke. No one has said her name in — in —

"Your . . . baby?" Nest whispers, and her eyes go to the rail, to the back of Owain ap Cadwgan cut harsh against the endless sky.

It's been three summers now. There was a time when I lived in terror of the thought of a baby and another when I was sure it would solve everything, but both were times when I actually believed it possible.

"Elen?"

Owain doesn't think on it at all.

"That day in the kitchen you asked me what I wanted. *She's* what I want." I scrub at my tears. "I want my sister back. Both my sisters. I want it *all* back and it's *never* coming back. Not my home. Not my parents. Not *anything*."

Nest pulls me under her arm and I let her. I let her because she says nothing while I cry, while the ship beneath us rolls back and forth like a cradle.

WE ARE DAYS ON THE SEA, BUT ONE MORNING, A TINY ridge of land edges onto the horizon. As we get closer, I can make out dozens of wharves crowded with sails and masts and brine-sleek ships of every color and size, and beyond is a town built tall that crawls with the kind of activity I've only seen in beehives. By midday, the cog is gliding up to a wharf, gentled forward or dragged slower in turns by oars, and sailors toss wrist-thick ropes to gangers to hold us fast.

Owain is last down the swaying ladder leading toward the wharf, and his feet have barely touched planks when Nest says abruptly, "We must go."

"Hush." Owain rubs his shoulder, scowling. "In a moment."

The sailors from our ship are lowering goods to men on the wharf or tossing them over the sides, chattering away in

Norse-Irish. One glances at us, then another, then the first makes a two-fingered gesture toward the town.

"No," Nest replies, sharp enough to bring Owain's head up. "We must go *now*. They mean to rob us."

Owain is instantly on guard, Einion penteulu and Rhys a blink behind. He sizes up the sailors, their shoulders big as horse haunches, the knives at their belts. Then he squints at Nest.

"Behind us," she whispers. "One's in a red tunic. The other has black hair. They have friends at the top of the wharf."

Owain presses a hand to his eyes. He's weary. We all are. Every muscle must work when you're on the sea. Your body doesn't know where it is, so it's always shifting trying to find out. You shiver every moment because you're damp enough to grow lichen on your back. There was never a time when Owain or Rhys or Einion penteulu was not standing watch, playing it off all friendly to the sailors, and there was never a time when I truly slept.

At length Owain makes the *scatter-and-regroup* gesture and mutters something in Rhys's ear. Einion nods and draws his blade behind his cloak while Rhys fights a pained look. Then we start up the wharf, me at Owain's elbow and Nest at Einion's with Rhys a half-step in front, for all the world just travelers leaving a ship.

"On my mark," Owain says to us sidelong, "girls with Rhys. Run hard. It might get bloody."

Rhael said they would not harm us if we gave them what they wanted. She said it as she pressed the fire iron in my hand,

and even then I wondered for those few fleeting instants why I would need it if there was no danger.

Footfalls behind us echo on wood. I'm still over green-black water deep enough to hold up a ship, and I still can't swim. We're halfway up the wharf when two big sailors step into our path. They're both smirking at Rhys, tall and reedy as he is, when Einion penteulu slams into the bigger one like a runaway ale wagon. Both sailors stagger back, and Owain hollers, "Go!"

I grapple Nest's hand and give Rhys the other as he shoulders past a sailor and deflects a grab for my hood. Somehow we get clear of the struggle — oh saints, it's bloody already — and hurry up a bustling wharfside alley lined with market stalls. Rhys drops my hand, but I hold tight to Nest's as we turn onto a broad street full of alewives and fishermen and apprentices and a curly-haired girl taunting a small boy with a fish head.

We pass at a rapid walk until the palisade gates flash above us and become toothpicks in the distance at our backs, and we're alone in a spring-greening countryside full of birdsong. In a short while Owain and Einion penteulu appear, and Rhys calls them over. They're panting, quivering, and wild-eyed, even coming at a dogtrot. This is a foreign land and we haven't been here long enough to piss, and already those two are shedding blood.

"Aww, sweeting, don't look at me like that," Owain says with a dredged-up smile. "Bastards had it coming. You saw it same as me." Then he glides past to where Nest curls against the hedge with her knees drawn up tight. He sits beside her and asks, "How did you know?"

"I . . . heard them." But it's blood in the water. She wasn't prepared to spin falsehoods, or she has no skill at it.

"I heard them too, chattering away like birds with four tongues," Owain replies, "but you *understood* them."

I see it in her face. Nest is wishing she'd let them rob us, stab us, and slide our bodies into the harbor. She didn't think. She just acted. Now Owain ap Cadwgan knows something she didn't want him to know.

"I did," Nest finally replies.

"How?" Owain asks, and his voice is mellow now, easy and coaxing.

She's deciding. Her sister's knife is buried to the hilt in his flesh and she's deciding whether to twist it or tend the wound. Whether she hates him more than she wants to live.

"My father bought the swords of the Norse-Irish many times to help his army." Nest says it low and fast. "My mother had a Dublin girl as a maid. I was often in her care. I understand much more than I can speak, though. It was many years ago."

Owain grins like a milk-fed cat. "And Einion here didn't want to bring you along. Saint Elen comes through for me yet again, though." He crosses himself and I smile, miracle-calm, even as things I can't say line up within me like masses for the dead.

Einion penteulu stands by the hedge nursing an eye that'll be purple before sundown and a slice across one cheek that could almost use irons. He snorts when I offer, shaking his head slow and insulted, like I'm the one who dealt him the cut.

AT LEAST ONE OF MY WORRIES IS FOR NOTHING. Finding the high king is as easy as asking the crofters and drovers we meet as we walk, and soon we're approaching the fort of Rathmore. I'm taken with how familiar it is. Had I not known better, I'd swear I was nearing Llyssun or Aberaeron. Same bristly rain-grayed palisades and well-guarded boundaries.

The Rathmore sentries approach, hands on weapons, and ask something in a hash of syllables. Owain mutters in Nest's ear, then guides her forward. She speaks to them, halting, like she's feeling along in a dark room. One of the sentries disappears, then returns with a woman who has silvery plaits and high freckled cheekbones. She's dressed in a fur-trimmed cloak and wears a horseshoe made of gold around her neck, and her tone is friendly and confident.

Owain looks at Nest expectantly, and she says, "The lady of this house is bidding us health in her lord's name, that we should come in and be welcome. She is called Sadb, and she is Muirchertach's wife."

Another of my worries, gone in a breath. After Owain's foot-dragging, I'd braced for a show of force from the Irish or at least a cold shoulder, Cadwgan's onetime allies or not.

"You must thank her," Owain replies. Nest says something to him, and he repeats it to Sadb sound for sound: *"Uh vwar vwugh."*

Sadb smiles and gestures for us to follow her through the gate and across a muddy courtyard toward a structure that must be the hall. Nest tries to drop back, away from Owain, but he puts her hand on his elbow and turns on her that feral warband smile that gives me the shudders. So I take her other hand as we slog through Rathmore's yard, and she presses so close that we bump shoulders every other step.

The hall is dim and smoky. There's a hearth and benches and trestle boards leaning against the wall. A cat hunches over a mouse near the door and two graybeards play flinches near the fire. I know this place is not Llyssun and the steward won't be speaking a tongue I can follow, much less have any stories of tiny Owain, but I still run my thumb along the door frame out of simple, wishful habit.

Sadb asks something of Owain, but he smiles graciously and motions to Nest. Nest's face reddens as she stumbles out some syllables to our hostess. Sadb nods, touches Nest's cheek in a kind and motherly way, then addresses servants who have gathered around her. A girl of about ten summers skips forward, and my first thought is to hug her because she and Margred could be sisters. She's sun-browned, like me, which makes her wheat-white hair stand out like a halo. Sadb puts a hand on the girl's head and says something like *orla*.

"Órlaith," Nest repeats, and the wheat-haired girl beams and pokes both thumbs into her chest.

Then Sadb says something to Órlaith, and Nest winces so hard I bite my tongue to keep from asking what she heard. Sadb notices Nest's expression and pauses, but Nest forces a smile and makes a helpless open-handed gesture. Órlaith tugs on my sleeve just like Margred does when she has something to show me. I hesitate, but Sadb shoos me with a patient smile before calling to someone else, so I let the child tow Nest and me away. I can only hope Rathmore's kitchen is as familiar as everything else so far. Perhaps there'll be a spare bladder and I can make the three of us a ball.

Behind the hall is a small shed with a curtain tacked across the door, and inside is a basin of clean water on a bench. A wooden dish of soap sits next to the basin, and a scrap of linen hangs from a peg jammed between the wall wattles. Órlaith makes motions like I should wash my face and body.

I blink back tears. I know I'm in a state. I know this is no way to present myself in anyone's hall, much less a king's, but I was dragged from my bed one morning and spent more days than I can count fleeing warbands who wanted Owain's head on a spear before being bundled onto a ship full of filthy cutthroats who pointed and leered when I pissed in a bucket behind my cloak. It's not like these people have to mock me for it.

Órlaith frowns thoughtfully, then holds up one finger and disappears.

Nest squirms. "Elen? I must beg your pardon. I think I may have told them something that isn't true. Not on purpose, though. I swear it."

"What? What did you tell them?"

Órlaith is back, and over her arm is a handful of new wool that tumbles into an elegant gown in a gray-blue that makes me think right away of the sea. She holds it out and in fearlessly bad Welsh says, "A gift from my lady. For the wife of the guest."

My mouth hangs open. Nest looks away.

"You have to tell them you were wrong," I whisper to Nest. "That I'm not really Owain's wife. What if he's furious?"

"I'm not sure I can! I told you, I understand a lot more than I speak. Besides, how can I, now? It'll look like I was lying. You think Owain ap Cadwgan will like that better?"

I have no wish to find out, so I make myself smile at the girl. I take the gown like it might burn. Órlaith grins, then hustles me behind the curtain and pulls it closed. Shadows of her bare feet move along the bottom edge. She must be standing watch outside, making sure I'm not disturbed. I strip down and wash every handswidth of my filthy, sweaty body. By the time I'm done, the water is gray and murky, but I'm pink with clean, smelling faintly of soapwort and lavender.

There's a shift to wear with the gown. It's made of soft linen with a tiny runner of embroidery around the collar. Órlaith brings me a pair of calfskin shoes made from leather so soft that I can't feel a single seam, then she sits me on a stool just outside the curtain and brushes my hair while the brittle spring sun puts a shine on it.

Mayhap it will be a good thing if the high king believes Owain is married. Then our host will see a fellow king's son and his wife and some retainers seeking refuge from the English king's overblown temper. Not a ragtag passel of troublemakers dodging well-deserved consequences by taking up lodging in his hall.

Too soon, Órlaith plaits my hair and pins it and tugs me gently to my feet. My whole scalp feels tight, and it makes me stand up straight and push my chin out.

"I get water for your cousin. I walk you in after." She gestures to Nest, leaning against the shed corner, then dumps the basin and heads toward the well.

Nest unwinds the tie from her plait and shakes her hair into stiff, wavy worms. "By the way, we're cousins now. I hope you don't mind gaining a relation." She sighs and adds, "I must ask your pardon. For all this. I'm not mocking you. I swear."

"I know. It's all right." My hair is arranged and braided, and I've no need to see it to know it looks proper. I'm wearing undergarments and shoes so beautiful that Owain would have to raid the Holy Land for something finer. There's not a hint of blood on this gown.

It's better than all right.

Órlaith returns with a basin of fresh water and Nest disappears behind the curtain. Then the girl takes my hand and pulls me toward the hall. Where the other wives will be gathered, and I don't have a word in Irish.

"I would wait for my cousin," I tell Órlaith, but she's having none of it as she leads me cheerfully toward the hall door. Perhaps she doesn't understand me. She's clearly excited, just like Margred gets when something new is happening. Digging in my heels like a mule would make me look unfriendly, and we must make a good impression since things got bloody on that Waterford wharf. All of us, especially the newly minted wife of Owain ap Cadwgan.

Near the hearth, two women sit on a bench with spindles paused in their laps. They have Nest's years and round, well-fed faces. Órlaith says something to them lordly and important, her chest puffed like a warhorse on parade. I catch Owain's name. The girl bows her head to the dark-haired woman at the end of the bench, then turns to me and says, "My lord's daughter. This is Aoife."

I should have insisted on waiting for Nest. She's a king's daughter, too. She'd know what to do—sit down with them? Curtsy? Introduce herself? She would say this woman's name right the first time, *Eee-fa,* and not stumble over the familiarity of it, calling a highborn lady she just met by her given name.

But Aoife rises and nods politely, then puts her spinning basket on the floor and moves enough to make a place for me to sit. Her companion chatters at me in Irish like I'm a saint who just appeared in a wisp of pink smoke, her spindle forgotten across her knees. Órlaith tries to make sense of their questions in her bits and pieces of Welsh, so I'm fairly sure that Aoife and her friend are wondering where we came from and how long we'll be staying and whether Einion penteulu has a wife — ha! — and not to mind the cat because he loves not knowing his place and how it would please them greatly if I'd spin with them.

This was Isabel once. She'd have stood before the likes of Gwerful and Annes, smiling bravely, not sure where to sit. Not sure what to say.

Aoife's friend is called Gormlaith. I must repeat it three times before I get it right: *Gor-em-lee.* She doesn't seem to mind, though. I take the spindle she offers and try to answer their questions. I'm fairly sure Órlaith makes things up when she cannot understand my answers. They keep smiling, though. Big and open, as if they're truly glad I'm here.

Soon, Órlaith bobs her head to Aoife and says to me, "I bring her." She bounces out the rear door, and it takes me a moment to realize she's checking on Nest in the bathing shed. I brace for the silence to be strained, but Aoife merely offers her basket of wool and gestures for me to take a handful. Gormlaith nudges me playfully and holds out a skein for me to admire. The cat climbs into her sewing basket, and Aoife rubs his ears. We run our spindles down our legs with the same practiced motion, and I smile at each of them in turn, like a proper wife might.

I don't see Owain till just before supper, when he trudges into the hall in the company of a cheerful young man who has years enough to be in a warband but clearly sees little of the practice yard. Owain is wearing a clean tunic with his hair damp and curly to his collarbones, but he's got a stiff, pained look about him, the look he wore at his father's wedding.

"Aoife says that lad is Niall, her foster brother," Nest whispers. "Apparently he loves visitors. Something about needing attention."

Owain hopefully mimics drinking, thumb to mouth and smallest finger jostling, but Niall is too excited to notice. He's already across the hall and beckoning Owain toward a group of well-dressed young men with nice posture gathered who look like they spend a lot of time indoors. Owain fights a scowl, but at length he sighs and joins Niall's friends. He's all charm as he greets them, but he fidgets with the elaborate Irish brooch pin at his shoulder like it's a millstone. When Niall finally does put a mug in his hands, Owain drinks the lot in four swallows, thrusts the mug back at Niall, and sighs like he's being made to sit through mass twice.

Aoife pats my knee and says something. Nest murmurs, "She hopes Niall will be a good companion for your, ah, *husband* while he's here."

I can think of no better company for Owain than a lad who appreciates relics and puts a polish rag to his boots now and then. Hopefully Aoife's foster brother likes hunting and hawking so Owain can spend his exile running down deer instead of helpless crofters and burning nothing but turf in a late-night fire and not thinking on why he's here in the first place.

At supper we are presented to our host, the king of Munster and high king of Ireland. Muirchertach Ua Briain is lean like a blade and has the look of a stable groom, but there is no question he is master of this hall.

When Owain kneels before him, Muirchertach grins and says in rusty Welsh, "Cadwgan ap Bleddyn!"

Owain flinches so slightly as he rises that I'm likely the only one who sees it. They do look alike, Owain and his father, and it must be both strange and wondrous to see so much of an old friend in his son. Owain presents the gifts, Nest at his elbow dredging up syllables and trying to look pleasant. I'm behind them, between Rhys and Einion penteulu. They're both clean-scrubbed and standing to, and even Einion is smiling in a way that doesn't make me want to slap him raw.

"Welcome!" Muirchertach gestures to an empty trestle opposite the high table.

Owain bows his head and says *"Uh vwar vwugh"* once more like he means it, but he moves past all of us, intent in that blank-eyed warband way. He throws himself down on the bench and seizes a haunch of mutton and a slab of eel pie as if this were Llyssun or Aberaeron. I look to Nest, but her eyes are on the ground and she's scurrying after Einion penteulu and Rhys as they make a more measured way toward the table.

Sadb is frowning and Muirchertach looks puzzled, like he

missed something. We must make a better showing than this. So I furl my skirts like I once saw Isabel do and walk steady and proper toward the empty place at Owain's right hand. More than one man watches me cross, and I even catch Rhys staring until he shakes hair over his eyes and studies the table grain.

Owain ap Cadwgan glances me up and down, then nods.

I pile some goose and turnips onto my plate, then add a steaming wedge of that pie. A servant pours me a mug of wine. I sit up straight and savor every flaky, salty mouthful. Whatever this is, it's definitely better than all right.

I daresay it might be what ordinary is supposed to look like.

We're given a bed. It's in a chamber across the yard set aside for guests, and it's stuffed with fresh straw and made up with a pile of furs and woolens. There's a thick curtain that shuffs on wooden rings when you draw it.

I must tell Owain what Nest said. It must be now, before he learns of it in some uncomfortable, damaging way, but he's shucking his fine new clothes hither-thither and growling how Niall should shut up about that pet magpie or he'll roast the damn thing in butter and eat it in the public of the courtyard.

So I unpin my hair, slide my thumb down each plait one by one, and shake them loose and ripply.

I've got Owain's attention.

Before long he's spent, and we're lying in tumbled bedclothes and he's playing with the ends of my hair while making an idle jest about the rumor of his sudden marriage sending Cadwgan to an early grave. I run my thumb over Owain's knuckles and spin out how useful it'll be for Muirchertach to believe him married. He'll seem steady, kingly even, and he doesn't need to lie, just not correct anyone and let the language bog do its work. By the time I draw the covers tight around my neck, Owain is repeating the notion as if he himself came up with it, down to using words like *kingly*.

†

ON MY FIRST DAY OF EXILE, I AWAKEN TO A BASIN OF
fresh water by the bed and Órlaith scratching at the curtain and
whispering, "I can help with your hair and dress?"

The hem of my gown has been scraped clean of mud and
spot-scrubbed so it's bluer than ever, and someone hung it on the
garment rod so nothing chewed it up during the night.

"You'll be all right, sweeting?" Owain is struggling into his
tunic. "I'm off to find Einion and Rhys, for I cannot bear to
spend — rot it to hell."

Niall stands outside the door that opens to the courtyard,
trying not to look in too purposefully or intently. I gather he's
been waiting on Owain, that there's a new water mill nearby
he's keen to show off. It's half a day's ride just to get there, and
there's a lovely monastery on the way where they keep annals.
Niall chatters brightly and draws curlicue shapes in the air,

mimicking illumination, and Owain bares that warband smile this lad doesn't know to fear.

"I'll be fine," I tell him. "Off you go. We mustn't be rude."

Owain muffles a groan but kisses me farewell. Niall looks away, pinkening, so Owain takes his sweet time and paws me up and down for good measure. When they finally do clatter out, I shoulder my rucksack, put on my new shoes, admire the stitching and the color and the dyework, then head to the maidens' quarters, where Nest has been given a bed.

No one answers my knock, so I let myself in. There are two rows of pallets with an aisle between them, and all are neatly made up and empty but for one near the door where Nest lies still and silent beneath a pile of blankets.

I hurry to her side. "Saints, are you all right?"

"Just tired." Nest doesn't turn to look at me, only pulls the covers more tightly around her neck.

Tired. My mother said that all the time when she was expecting Miv. "Ah . . . can I bring you something?"

"No. Thank you. I just want to rest. I'm sure it's merely the journey catching up with me. I'll be fine on the morrow."

"Very well." I wait, though. A moment, then another, in case she wants to say more. In case she wants to change her mind, because if she doesn't, I'll be without the one person who can help me be here.

But Nest stays still, eerily so, and at length I leave and shut the door firmly behind me. Outside, I lean against the wall of the maidens' quarters and press both hands over my eyes. I do not often trouble Saint Elen with prayers. Asking for more than I've been given is as bad as putting words in her mouth. Mostly what I do is thank her. This prayer's not for me, though. This one she is sure to look on kindly.

Please keep Nest from harm. All harm. Especially this harm.

I rock wearily away from the wall. Aoife and Gormlaith will be expecting me to pass the day with them. Nest being at my elbow would help, but they are waiting for the wife of Owain ap Cadwgan, not her. I smooth my skirts and make my way across the yard.

Aoife and Gormlaith are spinning when I edge close to the hearth. There's already a space on the bench for me. They look genuinely sorry when I tell them with gestures that Nest isn't feeling well, but they smile when I sit down with my rucksack. While we work, they teach me to say things in Irish. They giggle when I get words wrong, but not in a cruel way, and they squeal and clap when I say things properly, so I enjoy the learning as much as the knowing.

The cat saunters around my feet all morning, but by late afternoon, he perches imperiously on my lap with paws and tail tucked under so he looks like a loaf of fur. I start working on Margred's toy dog instead of spinning so I don't disturb his careful pose. If you bother this cat in any way, he sinks hidden claws into your leg, but he won't jump down till he's good and ready.

May 1110

It's sunny after a se'ennight of downpour.
There's no way I can spend another day indoors. Aoife and
Gormlaith agree. They've already got baskets packed, and they
point to the gate and the green countryside beyond. I wave them
ahead, shouldering my rucksack. If ever there was a day sure to
coax Nest from her stuffy little corner of the maidens' quarters,
it would be this one.

The door to the maidens' quarters is open, and as I near, a
graybeard in rich robes the color of good claret steps into the
entrance and holds a tiny glass vessel full of yellow liquid up
to the light. Inside, Sadb and Órlaith are standing over Nest's
pallet. Sadb is frowning like my mother would when Rhael or
I was down with some fever, and Órlaith is holding a tray piled
with meat and bread. Sadb asks the man something, and he takes
a tiny sip of the liquid, frowns, swirls what's left, then shrugs.

Órlaith spots me and approaches. She doesn't grin and bounce, and of everything wrong in this room, that makes my heart judder. She holds up the untouched food and says, "Your cousin doesn't eat. My lady is worried."

Oh saints. That man is a court physician.

I move past Órlaith and hurry toward Nest. Sadb steps aside so I can kneel at her head, but Nest pulls the blanket across her face.

"All I need is one more day of rest." Nest's voice is muffled by the wool. "I think I'm getting better. I'm just so tired."

You've been saying that for nearly a month. I bite it back. I don't want to use words like *month.* Instead I try, "It's beautiful out today. We're going to sit in the sun a while. You should join us."

"Next time."

Sadb and the court physician have moved toward the door, but she keeps glancing at Nest as they talk low and urgent. Finally she murmurs something to Órlaith, and the girl dutifully goes to Nest's side and kneels.

"My lord says . . ." Órlaith frowns thoughtfully, fishing for words. "Nothing in the piss. A woman thing, mayhap. He wouldn't know what."

Nest makes no reply, but my guts turn to ice. Órlaith rises with the tray and patters out behind Sadb and the court physician. Once the maidens' quarters are quiet, I whisper, "Please tell me this isn't what I think it is."

"I'm just tired. You should go. Aoife and Gormlaith are likely waiting."

I stand up slow. I turn my eyes Heavenward. Then I slip out the door.

Aoife and Gormlaith have spread a blanket on the ground beneath a stand of trees within an easy walk of the fort. By the time I reach them, I'm smiling like nothing's amiss, but my hands are shaking as I open my rucksack and pull out my spindle. Owain will find out soon. He knows Nest is ill and keeps to her bed. All that's left is for him to put the pieces together. He will smirk as her belly grows. The icing on his vengeance cake.

"Rawwwwr!" A cloaked figure leaps from the brush and lunges.

Aoife gasps, but Gormlaith snaps something violent and the figure throws back its hood to reveal a grinning young man. His hair is the color of foxes, and it leaps unkempt against the sky like a beacon. I've seen him around the hall, lurking in corners, pinching serving girls' backsides, farting at mass. Gormlaith scolds him roundly enough that I don't need any Irish to know she's blistering him, and the lad makes a rude gesture in a good-natured but mocking way. I catch what I'm fairly sure is a name—Cormac.

A handful of Irish lads appear out of the brush behind Cormac, all grinning like hounds. They're wearing long tunics and raggedy parti-color trews, and none of their cloaks have ever seen the inside of a laundry tub. Owain and Einion penteulu and Rhys are among them. Judging by the way they're jostling one another, packlike, obnoxious, they're up to no good, and we're their latest target.

When Gormlaith stabs a finger in Cormac's chest, his whole face darkens. He steps close and makes a taunting kissy-face down at her. Gormlaith stumbles back, wrenching her cloak over her chest. Cormac laughs, caustic, and Owain echoes him. The others join in, but Rhys nudges his hair over his eyes as he does it.

We're all on our feet now. My hand stings. I'm holding my spindle like a knife. Aoife folds her arms and asks something about Niall, haughty, but also the smallest bit hurt.

I frown at Owain. "Where is Niall? Did he not say—?"

"Is that any way to greet your beloved husband?" Owain palms my backside and smacks a noisy kiss on my lips.

"Owain!" I hiss, and he releases me abruptly, moving toward the pack of grinning lackwits who are already withdrawing into the brush they came from.

"What?" he asks, and before I can answer he turns to the lads and makes a whipcrack noise-gesture, and they snicker and jeer like I've been somehow made the fool.

I point incredulously at Aoife, who's the *daughter* of this house, and her foster brother has been kind enough to try to make Owain feel welcome, and all right, yes, it is a little ridiculous that Niall shrieks when he sees spiders and has an annoying habit of laughing at his own jokes, but he's no less a king's son for that.

Aoife repeats her question, her voice high and trembling, but when she mentions Niall, Cormac nudges Owain and mutters something that makes him cackle.

"*That's* what," I say through my teeth. "Niall told you at least three times that he thought it would be fun to —"

"How the hell should I know where that nuttering fool is?"

"Owain," says Cormac, and the tilt of his voice stretches the familiar sounds into something otherworldly. In choppy Welsh he goes on, "We bait them, townsmen. Good laugh to it."

Gormlaith looses a flurry of angry words that makes Aoife turn pink. Cormac laughs in her face and jerks a thumb over his shoulder, and the lads troop after him into the brush.

I snare Owain's sleeve. My spindle still held like a knife. "Where are you going?"

"You heard Cormac. We're going a-baiting. Mayhap I'll bring you back a tasty merchant to cook up for my supper."

"But — wait!"

Einion penteulu snorts. "It's just some harmless play, miracle girl. You're not worried something *ill* will befall us. Are you?"

I can't say that Owain promised his father he wouldn't give half a moment of grief to Muirchertach Ua Briain, who is both ally and friend, and this very much has the look of grief to it. I cannot tell him that none of this looks kingly, and I haven't spent se'ennights building us a place here for him to kick it down with thoughtless foolery.

I open my hand and Owain pulls free.

"Don't worry, sweeting." Owain grins over his shoulder as

he wades through the brush after Cormac, Einion penteulu and Rhys on his heels. "I'll be back by the time a husband's real work begins."

I watch him go. My face feels hot. Aoife tiptoes over, puts an arm around my shoulders, and says something in a comforting tone. She can't have followed the conversation in Welsh, so I must look as bad as I feel. Gormlaith makes a show of spitting, then hashes Cormac's name into a tirade. She takes my spindle, tosses it, then folds my hands into a vulgar gesture and holds them up high. I can't help but giggle. Then Gormlaith shoulder-bumps me into Aoife, who gives me a firm, fierce hug.

I may not be a wife in Powys, but with these girls for company, right now Isabel de Say ought to be envying *me*.

†

I LEARN THAT CORMAC IS THE YOUNGEST SON OF
Muirchertach's court bard. I learn he tricked Gormlaith into
sharing his bed last winter by hinting that he would marry her.
I learn he does not fight nor labor nor wear clerical cloth nor
follow any trade that I can tell.

I learn that if I ever need to find Owain, I must simply find
Cormac.

The more I learn of Cormac, the more he feels familiar, like he
could be beaten into Owain's warband on the morrow. We are far
from a place Owain has sway, though, and Cormac is neither a
brother in arms nor a brother in blood.

It's not long before Owain takes to sneaking out of bed at
cockcrow, leaving me to manage Niall appearing at the chamber
door with horses standing saddled behind him. Niall is always
earnest, fighting a look of bewildered hurt as he asks where

Owain has gone so early and without taking a meal. I can't bring myself to be truthful. Niall's good-natured innocence makes him trust too easily, and he is trying very hard to be a good host and befriend Owain. So I tell him I don't know where Owain has gotten to. I pretend my Irish is worse than it is. I shrug and smile, and Niall goes pink and nods and shuffles off.

In a way, though, saying I don't know is as true as I can make it. Owain is vague as to where he and Cormac and the rest spend their days, regardless of how I ask. Besides, after Cormac and his wolves barricaded Niall in the yard privy and bellowed with laughter as he banged on the door and all but wept for help, I'm not sure Niall truly wants to know where they are.

One morning, I step into the yard and Niall is not by the door. When I get to the hall, he's coaxing his magpie to lift its little feet to the tune a boy plays on a pipe whistle while an admiring crowd of youths oohs and aahs. Aoife cuts off my attempt at an apology by dropping the cat on my lap and insisting there's nothing to beg pardon for. Or mayhap she's saying the apology isn't mine to make.

Aoife doesn't say it coldly, but I spend the rest of the day with a tight ball of worry in my belly. Later, after Owain has rolled in long past dark and fallen into bed and pressed up close, I say, "Niall has been nothing but kind to you, and all you do is slight him. People have noticed."

"Slight him?" Owain scoffs. "He should be glad I'm a guest here or he'd know what I really think. Hell, what kind of man takes so many baths and carries a psalter?"

One who doesn't smell like sweaty horse and prefers not to linger in purgatory. But I bite my lip and say, "It's not just Niall. Had you been here today, you'd know Muirchertach went to parley with the men of Waterford again because they are weary of *certain bastards* sowing their cargos with live mice and waving bare buttocks at their wives."

Owain snort-cackles, like he's remembering it fondly. "If the men of Waterford return the favor, you'll be tempted to choose a pointy rock, but you'll do better with a nice round one. Aim true and put your weight behind it."

I sigh in disgust and shift away from him.

"What? No wife of mine is going to pass up a chance like that, is she?"

He's lucky there are no rocks at hand now. "Look, tomorrow there's to be a horse race. That could be fun, yes?"

"At Rathmore?" Owain's good cheer is gone in a moment. "No. I can't be here."

"But—"

"But nothing." He rolls over and puts his back to me. "Believe me, sweeting, it's best for all of us if I'm anywhere else as much as possible."

Anywhere else would be one thing, but not when it means out with Cormac stirring up hell in the Irish countryside. It would be different if they were a proper warband. Raiding has a purpose. Whatever this is will lead only to bad blood and bad ends.

After the room has gone quiet and there are no sounds but

the mice in the walls, I close my eyes and whisper my old prayer to Saint Elen.

> *Thank you for understanding.*
> *Thank you for everything you've done for me.*
> *Please make Owain see how dangerous this foolishness*
> *is so he'll stop—*

"What was that?"

I startle and nearly fall out of bed. Owain has risen on one elbow and now he's squinting at me in the slivers of moonlight from the half-closed window.

"N-nothing," I stammer. "I thought you were asleep."

"You said something about Saint Elen." Owain's voice is curiously level and wide-awake. "What she should do. I heard you."

My heart is hammering. I haven't said her name since the start of my prayer. Which means he's been listening to me, silent as a cat on the hunt, as I whispered all kinds of things in the dark. Carefully I reply, "I'm praying to her. She's my name saint."

I wait. Holding my breath. Owain beside me drawn tight like a bowstring.

At length he mutters, "I'm losing patience with exile. Not understanding what the hell anyone is saying. Having to ask for everything. People *expecting* things of me. All I want is to go home and take back what's mine. I'd listen to the Adversary himself if he'd give me a way to do it."

I shudder. It's too close to true.

"But I'd rather listen to a saint," Owain adds quietly.

I don't wait for the patter. I need him off this idea that he can have any sort of guidance from Saint Elen. I need him off it right now. "I wouldn't trust Madog ap Rhirid to govern a byre. Who does he think he is, trying to run a province like Powys?"

It lands where I mean it to, and soon Owain lies growling at the ceiling and the Almighty and whoever else is listening, which is me, because it's always me.

But now he's talking about what he plans to do. Recall the lads of his warband. End his cousin in a variety of gruesome ways. Things he means to do himself alone, without any help from Saint Elen.

It's suppertime. It's just like any of the meals at any of the halls in the kingdoms of Wales, only I'm at a proper place before a dish of hammered copper piled with meat and savories. Only I'm wearing glorious shoes and undergarments without a single tatter. Only the lord of this place has welcomed me in and sat me at this very table.

The sole thing that's the same is that everyone is looking at me and speculating.

I smile. I keep my head high. I bring food to my mouth bite by bite like nothing is wrong. Like Owain didn't bloody well promise he'd be at supper. Like I didn't bloody well believe him.

At the high table, Sadb and Muirchertach sit closer than they need to and share a cup of wine. Niall feeds tidbits to the magpie perched on his shoulder, and Aoife catches my gaze and rolls her eyes at him just the smallest bit like I'm sharing her joke at her elbow and not across the room. There's a place for Nest at my right, but it's empty because she's still only picking at the trays they send her in the maidens' quarters.

I'm merely tired. Please, just let me rest.

There's a massive thud, then a scuffle. Then singing. Loud, tomcat singing in Irish.

Sadb's color is rising. She leans into Muirchertach and asks if that's who she thinks it is, and he nods grimly.

There are another few thuds and some lackwit snickering, then Cormac and Owain stumble into the hall. They look like they've been digging turf all morning and fighting to keep it all afternoon. The other lads crowd the doorway, jostling and whisper-chortling but not daring to cross the threshold. Muirchertach rises, slow and ominous, hands in fists like ox hooves. He asks them with very brittle courtesy what in the name of every saint they mean by coming into his hall in such a state and thinking to take a meal.

Cormac makes a flourishing gesture and pulls Owain abreast of him, and they both kneel, still giggling like fools.

I put down my meat knife. Fold my hands in my lap.

Muirchertach makes an impatient gesture and they rise. They head for the guest table, but the high king growls that Cormac should get the hell out of his sight *right bleeding now* if he knows what's good for him. Cormac veers toward the door where the others are gathered, still giggling, and the lot of them wisely disappear. Muirchertach stabs a finger at Owain, then at the empty place next to me.

Aoife traces her meat knife in slow, winding loops across her mutton. Her cheeks are red. Niall regards me with open pity. Owain climbs over the bench with a swagger and runs a hand up my thigh under the trestle board. He smells like wind and heather and something else, something sharp and thin and vaguely grainy.

There's space at the end of the bench at the high table next to Aoife. I can't get up, cross the hall, and sit shoulder to shoulder with her, even though we could laugh about the cat singeing his tail on a stray hearth coal and share a big wedge of honey cake while her brother spoils a magpie and her parents trade kisses when they think no one is watching. I can't get up with bread in both hands and share it with Nest in the quiet of the maidens' quarters.

Instead I sit next to Owain ap Cadwgan in a pretty gown that did not come to me through violence, embroidery at my neck and calfskin on my feet, while knives snick through meat and ale is sipped and bread is torn in a newly uncomfortable hall.

I do it in silence, like a proper wife.

June 1110

On my way to the privy, I spot Nest by the gate. She's hooded and half in shadow, speaking intently with a graybeard who favors his right side and has a deep gash down his jaw. I rush toward her. She's on her feet for the first time since April. Perhaps she's ready to talk. To tell me in words what both of us know is happening.

Nest startles when I grab her hands and hold on. I want to beg her pardon. I want to cry. Instead I whisper, "You have no idea how glad I am to see you up and about."

The graybeard grunts and holds out a weathered palm. Nest slips one hand out of mine, reaches into her apron, and presses something round and shiny against the graybeard's fingers. He flips it, squints at it, then bites it. A coin.

Nest just gave silver to a fighting man.

"Yes. About that." There's no wavery choke in her voice now. No weak sighing. Her skin is fresh and ruddy. Not sickbed pale. "It's time you knew."

"Wait. Wait. You were ill. All these se'ennights. You were . . ." I hold my arms out over my belly, and Nest makes a face like I pissed in her porridge.

"Guh. I know. I'm sorry. I had to let you think it, though. If you didn't believe, none of the others would."

My mouth is slowly falling open. She's been planning this. All those picked-at trays of food. Keeping the bedcovers over her face. Her one complaint—*so tired*—something no one could challenge her on. Little wonder the court physician could find nothing wrong. Because there *is* nothing wrong. There never has been.

Now Nest has given money to a man who's clearly fought in more than one warband, and there's but one reason she'd do it.

She means to have Owain killed.

There's nothing to stop her now. Her children are safe. She's far from anyone who might rescue her. If she hires an assassin, chances are good she'll be successful. She can kill him and he'll be dead.

I glance at the hall where Aoife and Gormlaith are likely wondering what's keeping me, then I gesture for Nest to come behind the kitchen into a patch of ill-smelling shade. I'm too relieved to be angry she lied. I'm more worried about that gray-beard and the big knife at his side, how he's on his home ground and Owain is far from his teulu.

When Nest hesitates, I grab her arm again. My hand closes around something metal. I shove her sleeve up, and there's the bracelet Owain gave me. The one that was Nest's, from her father.

"You *stole* that from me!" I never wanted the bracelet at all, but she went through my things. The few things that are mine.

"I only borrowed it. I was going to give it back."

"How?" I square up like one of the lads. "That's not how these things work, you know. Once you pay a man to do a job, he tends to keep what you give him."

"Lower your voice!" she hisses. "It's not what you think."

"Look. Surely we'll be back in Wales soon." I'm fighting for calm. "Cadwgan is sure to send for Owain any day, either to move against Madog or because this whole thing has been settled. Then Cadwgan will see to it that you're back with your little ones like he promised. They've got to be missing you to bits."

Nest's face goes hard. "Owain ap Cadwgan is never going to let me go. You know that, don't you?"

There was no reason to bring Nest with us into exile. No reason but one: Cadwgan demanded that Owain release her to Gerald. In public. In front of everyone. That moment alone would have been enough, but Owain still has one eye to vengeance that can't be had without her. I nod miserably.

"God knows my husband can do little for me while I'm in Ireland. He might not even know where I am, or if I'm alive." Nest sighs, long and shuddery. "That means I must look to myself if I want to get clear of Owain ap Cadwgan."

"Get clear of—you're not planning to have him killed?"

Nest cracks a grim smile. "Tempting. But no. Too risky, and it won't get me what I want."

"Your babies," I whisper, and she chokes on a buried sob.

"That graybeard with the scar? He fought for my father in one of his hired armies. He agreed to see me home out of respect for my father's memory and for a big reward of silver that my husband will trip over himself to provide. That's why I had need of your bracelet. As proof of my blood. But here."

Nest fumbles it off her wrist, and I will not think of my father, who never in his whole life had two coins to rub together, as I push it back into her hands. "Just don't let Owain see it."

She drops it into her apron and holds a hand against it. "I'd get you clear, too. I'd have you come with me. Mayhap you can't have back what Owain ap Cadwgan and his lot took from you, but you can have a family—mine. It can be ours."

I fall against the kitchen wall and let it hold me up.

"William's already claimed you." Nest smiles halfway, sheepish. "Do you know he slept with the bladder ball you gave him tucked under his arm every night? I suspect he still does. I don't even want to think what'll become of David should *Alice* never come back. You always knew what to say to them, even when things were . . . bad." She swipes at tears, then flutters an awkward smile. "You'll live in our house. You'll be their nurse. When they're grown, you will be my companion. Unless you choose to marry. Even then you won't be rid of me. I will expect spiced wine when I visit."

A cozy chamber. Playthings scattered around. Not Miv's tiny

fingers winding through my hair. William bouncing his ball to David, who catches it with both hands because his comfort rag is stowed somewhere for safekeeping. A place where Margred can visit all the time because it won't matter whose sister she is.

". . . before the se'ennight is out," Nest is saying. "Will you come?"

"I . . ." I look over my shoulder at the hall, then down at my lovely, well-stitched shoes. "I like it here."

Nest sighs. "Oh, child, of course you do, but you being a wife is a playact, same as me wasting away in the maidens' quarters. It's not real."

"My gown is real. My shoes are real. It's all real. It's *ordinary*."

"You're playing house. Owain ap Cadwgan is not. He hasn't played for a moment while he's been here, and he definitely won't play once you're back in Wales."

"Let's not forget which of us told Sadb I was Owain's wife in the first place," I reply through my teeth, "and which of us sold him that not-real made-up story before he could think it through so he wouldn't get us run out of Rathmore in disgrace."

"Believe me, I haven't forgotten," Nest says, quiet and sharp. "This is my fault. I should have told Sadb the truth right away, but you . . . lit up, putting on that gown. You moved differently. Spoke more easily. Smiled like you meant it. Like all at once you were in command of the room. In command of yourself." She shakes her head and sighs. "I thought for sure that's what you'd walk away with. How it feels to belong. That this is who you are, and how you got here doesn't matter. I meant to do you a kindness. Not give you a shovel and stand by as you dug a deep hole."

I look down at my dress. My shoes. I blink hard.

Nest puts her arm around my shoulders like she did on the sea crossing. "Come with me. By the time he realizes we're gone, we'll have put foot on shipboard, and there's nothing on Heaven or earth that'll let him catch us. I'll be back with my husband, you will be nurse to my children, and I will actually pity Owain ap Cadwgan if he happens within a stone's throw of Gerald of Windsor for the rest of his natural life."

"You've forgotten what I am to Owain," I reply quietly, "and how he repays betrayal, be it real or in his mind."

"I thought you'd be pleased. That you'd *want* to be their nurse."

"I want a lot of things I can't have, but there's one thing I want that I *can* have. William and David and . . . and the baby, I want them to be safe. If I go with you, none of us will ever be safe."

Nest takes my hand. "Gerald will protect you. I know he will. In fact, Gerald will welcome you if by sheltering you he can tweak Owain ap Cadwgan's nose. Or lure him close."

"No." I pull away from her. "No, I'll not be part of anything that puts Owain in harm's way."

She groans faintly. "He's done nothing to earn your loyalty. He does less to keep it."

"It has nothing to do with loyalty."

"Not loyalty," Nest says slowly, puzzling, "and not love, either. Then . . . what?"

The patter rises to save me, but it's hard to make it hold water when there is Nest and her silver-hungry warbander and the promise of the little ones at the end of the voyage, and before, there was only Owain ap Cadwgan holding out his hand.

"Will you at least think on it?" Nest whispers. "I don't think I can face them if you're not with me."

I nod. I let her slip away toward the maidens' quarters believing it to be true.

†

I'{s} late. The sleeping chamber is still and dark. I'm alone in bed. If I peek through the curtain, I can see the faint glow beneath the door that leads to the yard. Owain and the lads are still at their fire, where they've been all evening and long into the night. It'll be Saint John's Day soon, and that means Cormac has escapades from last year to top. Gormlaith has let exactly what those might be sink into the language bog, and Aoife went white to the ears when I even mentioned the Feast of the Baptist.

There's a faint burst of laughter. I throw the covers back, pull on the bedrobe Aoife gave me, and slide my feet into my shoes. They feel cold and gritty without hose as I tiptoe to the door and look out. Near the palisade wall, Cormac and Owain are holding court, lit orange by firelight, passing wineskins and smaller vessels of the strong stuff that makes them particularly ugly.

Sadb pulled me aside before supper to tell me Órlaith wouldn't be plaiting my hair or bringing water or even setting foot in the sleeping chamber anymore. The child is frightened, Sadb said. She comes from a decent family. A king's son should know to keep better company.

It could be months before Cadwgan sends for Owain. Muirchertach Ua Briain may be an ally and a friend, but he's not a saint or a fool.

The lads are comparing spoils as I edge near. Cormac has a girl's undershift smudged with grass stains. Owain has a long hank of blue-black hair bound with a leather strip. Einion penteulu has what I hope is a pig's ear. Rhys notices me first. He nudges Owain with the hinged lid of a jewelry box he's holding, and when Owain spots me he grins in a slow, lazy way. He's the kind of drunk that only comes from settling into a flagon in midafternoon.

"Sweeting, it's cold. Go inside."

"I will, but . . . when are you coming to bed?"

Cormac says something about fillies and riding, and the Irish lads all snicker. For once I'm glad I understand little of what's said to me, especially when it's said quickly. Owain smirks at them and makes a helpless, apologetic gesture, then rises and pulls me a pace away.

"What is it?" he asks in a low voice, clear and steady, and all at once I wonder if I was wrong about him being drunk.

"I—I just wondered where you were."

"Well, now you know. So go back inside." He glances at the

lads, who watch us, slumped and giggle-drunk, like we're a bear-baiting. Or a hanging.

"I just . . ."

"She just wants to know where you *are*," Einion penteulu simpers. "At all *times*. Like a *wife* might."

Owain laughs aloud. I try to swallow the choke in my throat, but I cannot. I can't even look at him.

Einion shakes his head, slow and disgusted. "I told you this would happen if you didn't kill that marriage lie outright. Next thing you know, she'll whisper in your ear that the likes of us are making you grieve our host like your father warned you against. She'll pull you onto her lap like a good little dog and wind up the leash."

"It was a misspeaking, not a lie." Owain lifts his brows. "Right, sweeting?"

I swipe at tears. That misspeaking is the one thing that might make Owain behave himself here. That could repair what's already been damaged. I stare at my feet and say nothing.

Einion penteulu makes a lordly *told you so* gesture into the silence.

"Jesus wept." Owain presses his hands to his forehead. "So that's what this is. You and everyone else in this whole place would have me dance like a trained bear. The high king, because I'm to be my father's son. His wife, because apparently any sort of amusement in her household is ruinous. And you, because of one misplaced word from *months* ago. By Christ, I seem to remember being promised trickery that could only help me."

I straighten. "It is—"

"It is *not!*" Owain cuts in. "It's *humiliating*, being here. Sitting at another man's table. Eating his meat. Sleeping in a bed that's not mine, beneath a roof that'll never be mine. *Nothing* helps with that. I hope you're getting something out of your little ploy, sweeting, for I'm sure as hell not."

"It might help," I stammer, "if you'd let it."

"My lackwit cousin is running my inheritance into ruin. My father crouches like a whipped hound before the English king. Here I am, apparently the only one who sees what must be done and has the stones to do it, expected to fill my days with useless horseshit while my birthright slips away a little more each godforsaken hour. If that's not enough, you're out here clutching at my hem before all these men and begrudging me a little harmless play."

I was ready to withdraw. Smile big, kiss his cheek, let him save face in front of his foster teulu and let them watch me walk away. Instead I bark a harsh laugh. "So it's hard, is it? Being under someone else's roof when you'd rather be home? Expectations you don't know what to do with? Always on tiptoe, never at ease? And never is it far from your mind that your full belly and warm back depend on the goodwill of one man?"

Owain frowns, cocks his head.

But Einion penteulu sighs like a bellows. "Christ Jesus, lass. That was *years* ago. Besides, it's not like you didn't come out of it well."

Cormac makes the whipcrack noise-gesture, slow and

taunting, and as the rest of them laugh, Owain lets go of my arm and rejoins the flickerlit circle.

"Go inside." He puts his back to me. "There's no place for you here."

I go inside. There's little else to do.

I don't sleep, though. I lie fully clothed beneath the covers, trembling. One misplaced word from months ago and here I am, still playing house. Waiting in bed, like a proper wife.

For three years now I've spun falsehoods and told myself they were for Owain ap Cadwgan. I should know lies for what they are. How the most tempting of them glitter and shine. How easy it is to believe when you have every reason to want it so.

The pallet shifts like someone is leaning against it. Nest's whisper glides through the dark. "Are you awake?"

I could say nothing. Pretend to sleep. Heaven knows Nest did enough of that in the last few months. Only I am alone, and nothing will ever be ordinary. "Yes."

"Can I stay a while? They've gone . . . out."

I throw the bedclothes back, and she slides in beside me. She presses her shoulder against mine as if we really were cousins and sharing space in the maidens' quarters. Like Margred and I sometimes did for hours at a stretch on lazy afternoons, *just like sisters,* she'd say, with the cozy delight of someone who had none by birth. She'd whisper what to a child passed for secrets, and my whole heart would hurt at how innocent some girls get to be.

At last I whisper, "You were right. It *is* just a playact. A *misspeaking*. I'm a fool for thinking it anything more. It should have worked, though. With the right idea in his ear . . . but he's no different than he is at home. If anything, he's worse."

"He's no different," Nest replies. "You are."

Drunk or sober, Owain speaks of little now but going home. How it'll be. His warband recalled. His cousin slain. His father shown up and proved wrong. His birthright secured and everything just as it was. Just as it should be.

Which means every holiday will look like Christmas at Aberaeron. Isabel's cruel smile and Cadwgan's sidelong disdain. Easter and Michaelmas, Whitsuntide and Candlemas. Every fort like the one before, only Margred will never be there. She'll refuse to come near the man who killed her brother, even for me. She will grow up and take her place among the wives who ignore me, and in fort after fort I'll spin quietly in some dim corner and wait alone for Owain to come back, grinning and blood-spattered and loaded down with plunder while men like Gerald of Windsor wait for him deep in the greenwood. If I'm lucky, if my playact holds, back will come Owain ap Cadwgan to wherever he's decided there is a place for me. He'll slip some shiny thing over my wrist, still warm from the girl it was taken from, and he'll grin like a wolf and pass the meat and take me to bed and bloody well praise himself for what a good man he is.

"I'm leaving on the morrow." Nest speaks low. "I'd still have you come with me. My children love you, and that makes you part of my family. Just like you were blood."

I told them to stay together. I told them I'd be back, that I'd

195 •

always come back. David clung to my cloak-end and William pulled it from his grip, clear and confident and steady, and told him not to be afraid.

"All right," I whisper, and under the covers Nest takes my hand and holds it tight.

It's not like you didn't come out of it well.

A clatter in the dooryard. Rhael and me shoulder to shoulder, her breath fast and shallow.

After Nest returns to the maidens' quarters, I reach between the pallet and the wall and pull out Owain's rucksack. I paw through his tunics and underclothes till I find his dagger with the hammered bronze sheath. I take it, as well as the silver torc that Owain was to give to Cadwgan upon his return, a gift from his old brother in arms. Then I pull out the heavy gold ring that was Owain's grandfather's and the plain leather purse that's heavy with coin.

Four-and-ten-year-old me slowly unwinding the last bandage from Owain's healed wound. Wrung out from nightmares. Perched stiff on the edge of the bed and reminding herself that this is what she asked for. This is a thing she can somehow do.

It's not like you didn't come out of it well.

Once I asked Saint Elen for my life and she gave it to me, but when someone gives you something, it does not really become yours. The giver still decides when and why and how. And a gift can always be taken back.

I bundle the knife, the ring, the torc, and the purse into my own rucksack, tight so they don't clank and betray themselves valuable. Then I drink a whole wineskin of thrice-brewed ale, undress, and crawl under the bedclothes.

When you take something with your own hands, that's when it becomes yours.

It's the darkest part of night when I wake up needing a piss. Owain beside me lies asleep. Naked, sprawled, taking up most of the bed and all the bedclothes. Snoring like an elderly hound. Smelling faintly of spirits.

I think of the dagger. For many long moments.

I slip out of bed and dress, then sling my kitful of plunder over one shoulder. I leave my spindle, though. I've spun enough falsehoods to last all my life.

IT'S NOT MORNING YET FOR ANYONE BUT THE POOR
scullions kindling the day's first fires—and a single scarred graybeard pretending to fish leaves out of the common trough. Nest
emerges from the maidens' quarters, hooded like a leper, and
heads toward the graybeard like she's got nothing to hide. I pull
up my own hood and fall into step beside her. Our feet pad in
steady unison like a team of horses.

The graybeard squints at me, then Nest. He says something
to her, measured, something about silver, and Nest pours out a
string of syllables that ends in *Gerald of Windsor*. The graybeard
sighs, low and long-suffering, but nods us toward the gate and
mutters for us to keep our faces in shadow. As the sentries slide
the heavy bar out of the notches, Einion penteulu stumbles out
of the yard privy, staggers, and leans hard against the building
like someone poured him there.

I face away. Too fast. Too sudden. I've drawn his attention. I can feel it.

There's no way I can go back. No way to replace all the things I took exactly where I found them. Owain will notice. He'll want to know why. He will come to conclusions that will be absolutely and unmistakably correct.

"What is it?" Nest's voice is a calming murmur. A mother's voice. I will not think of my mother.

"Einion ap Tewdwr. He saw us. He'll tell Owain."

"Shh. He saw nothing. It's early. He's tired and probably drunk." Nest looks over her shoulder, though.

The gate creaks open enough to step through, and we're outside and moving toward Waterford at a walk too fast to be seemly.

Barely a threemonth. I was still counting the days. At not-quite-dawn, I slid past a dozing sentry and fled in no direction. Just *away*. I stumbled through the dark until I fell over something and my ankle twisted wrong and I couldn't stand up true for anything. Einion ap Tewdwr came upon me where I lay curled among the roots of a massive oak. I braced for the grab, hard to the ground *can't struggle,* but he merely leaned down and whispered in my ear.

We killed them both and seized all the beasts.

It was enough. The bulk of him, the creak of leather armor and the faint whiff of sweat on sweat. It was enough to break me, and I followed him back without a word, hobbling hard because I would not take his arm.

Einion had not made the brutes let me up for my own sake while Owain lay bleeding, but a fighting man should have realized how saving someone's life binds you together in a way that goes deeper than blood.

Mayhap he did not think. Mayhap he only acted.

The sky is almost pink when we arrive at the Waterford wharves. The graybeard brings Nest and me to a ship, and the three of us board and move to the rear. All that's left is to wait for the tide.

Around us, the sailors prepare for the voyage. Slowly it occurs to me that this is really happening. We are getting clear. Soon I'll see the little ones again. They will be safe and whole. There'll be games of border raids. Whole afternoons to play at ball. Cozy evenings perfect for my mother's stories. William and David and Not Miv were never supposed to love me, but they do.

This is how you make a place. This and no other way.

We've just cast off when there's a clamor on the wharves and the sailors stop their sail hauling and oar wrangling to shout at the gangers who are flagging them down. After a scuffle with ropes and a scrape and a thud, another passenger climbs aboard, appearing over the side of the ship hand over hand.

Oh, Jesus wept. It's Rhys.

I pull my hood sharp across my face and watch him sidelong as he scans the deck. He's come to bring us back. Einion penteulu wasn't as drunk as Nest thought. Owain must know everything, including the fact that his rucksack has been emptied of valuables and there can be but one culprit.

Nest nudges me and mutters in a gruff boyish voice, "Eyes down."

The ship takes on that drop-sway feeling that only comes from being on water with nothing below but a few planks of wood and the breath of the saints. The wharf creeps past in slow, maddening handswidths.

Hurry. For God's sake.

A sailor approaches Rhys and gestures to the back of the ship. Rhys shakes his head and steps around the sailor toward some piled cargo. The sailor shoves him toward the rear, and Rhys staggers, then falls into a fighting crouch and garbles something in bad Norse-Irish about a king's son and missing girls.

The oars plash beneath us.

Faster. Please.

Two more sailors appear. I will Rhys to stand down. To rethink what he means to do. He's here at Owain's bidding, but that doesn't mean I want to watch this crew beat the stuffing out of him, even if it takes long enough for wind and tide and oars to put some water between the ship and the wharf.

The captain approaches and speaks to Rhys in broken Welsh. "Passengers to the stern."

"Two girls," Rhys says impatiently. "Are they on board? If they are, you'll have to turn around. It's life and death."

The captain laughs and gestures to Nest and me and the graybeard. Nest squeezes my hand. Her face is stone. The graybeard frowns at the commotion but makes no move.

Rhys squares up. His hair is close-cropped like Einion

penteulu's now, and without it to hide behind, he is nowhere near the boy who worried over Normans or thought to protest minding me. "Turn *around*. At the word of a king's son."

"The tide obeys no man's son." The captain folds thick brown arms. He's broad like a barrel and missing half an ear. "It's running now, and I'm for Wales. Passengers to the stern. Or overboard. Take your choice."

Rhys groans low at the wharf growing smaller against Waterford. He glances at the small rowboat overturned near the mast, then at the sailors keeping a wary eye on it and him. At length he curses and sways toward us, stepping around cargo and falling over ropes.

The graybeard drops a hand to his knife-hilt, but Nest says to Rhys in a calm, cheerful voice, "You're too late, lad. We've slipped loose of the tether by fair means. Go take a seat before this man hurts you badly." Rhys's face gets redder by the moment, and Nest goes on, still light and friendly. "Do please have a care how you speak to us. This man may not understand what we're saying, but he'll gut you like a fish should he think you mean us harm."

"I'm more than willing to leave you to him." Rhys matches Nest's pleasant tone. "She's the one I was sent to fetch back." He twitches his fingers at me. Like he might to a reluctant hound.

I link arms with Nest.

"Oh, Christ Jesus. You cannot be here willingly. No." Rhys's voice goes faint. "I didn't believe him. Einion penteulu thinks very little of you. I was sure someone meant Owain harm. Make him vulnerable, then . . ."

I cough a quiet laugh. Right. God forbid I go missing and Owain's the one to worry about.

"Your loyalty speaks well of you," Nest says to Rhys, "but you'd best steel your guts to stand before Owain ap Cadwgan with the word that he'll have to do without a saint now."

"Oh no, I'll not." Rhys replies, but he only speaks to me. "You're going back to Owain. He will not die because of you. I will not have it."

Nest folds her arms. "I don't give half a damn what you'll have. I do give half a damn what *Elen* will have. So know this. When we land, my husband will be waiting. Elen and I will go with him. You will cheerfully bid us good health, or I swear before every last one of the saints you will not live to draw your next ten breaths, much less return to Owain ap Cadwgan with this news."

"We'll see," Rhys says quietly, and he nods to the graybeard and takes a seat opposite us. The graybeard grunts and makes a show of toying with his weapon. He's taking no chances, and I'm glad for it.

Rhys catches my eye and makes the field gesture for *betrayed,* then stabs a finger toward Ireland growing small and dark in the distance. I look away, not from shame like he'd have it, but to his arm that I healed, and I grit my teeth against tears that make no sense. *Betrayed.* Rhys has been nearly a year in Owain's warband.

More than enough time to watch and learn, to listen to men he's desperate to earn a place among. To take in the playact as I spun it out. Of course he thinks I've betrayed Owain. It's that simple to him.

My hands want to make *betrayed* back at Rhys, but I didn't heal his wound so he'd owe me something. I hoped for belief and I got it. Expecting anything else from the lads will leave me disappointed every time. Even one so young he has no need of a razor, who's been given the chance to win his spurs by fetching me back.

Even one who still has the use of both arms because of me.

I hope for fair winds to speed us home. Once we land, I will only ever face forward. If Saint Elen truly has been looking to Owain all these years, she might keep at it for reasons beyond my understanding. If she hasn't, he's no worse off than he was the moment ere he kicked in my door.

I gesture *stand down,* and Rhys snorts and turns away. One of us is going to be left high and dry at the end of this voyage, and I've come too far for it to be me.

†

RHYS STAYS CLOSE. THE SHIP IS THIRTY PACES LONG, and he can hardly sit elsewhere, but it's clear he does not mean to return to Owain empty-handed. Rhys is broader now, less stringy, but he must know he alone is no match for whatever force Gerald of Windsor will bring to the wharf.

That means he has a different plan.

We awaken one morning to find the ship riding the wind toward a smudge of town, pushed by the morning tide. The cog anchors when it's still a ways offshore, and sailors ready the row-boat. Nest starts toward it, but the graybeard tells her to wait. She fidgets and stands at the rail as sailors lower the boat and the oarsman rows it toward town.

Nest shades her eyes with one hand, but nothing's out of the ordinary on the wharves. Just seabirds and masts and gangers at their labor.

Then a crowd beings to gather. Men and horses. Enough to make a warband.

After a long while, the rowboat pulls back across the harbor. The sailor hauls himself on board, tells the captain that everything is in order, and hands the graybeard a heavy leather purse. The graybeard peers inside, then throws three handfuls of silver pennies into a strongbox held out by the captain's penteulu.

Gerald's coin is real. He's on the wharf. Soon I'll be with them again. Warm and squirmy, smelling of porridge and soap.

The graybeard points at Nest, then the rowboat. She all but dances toward it, but when I move to follow, a redheaded sailor puts himself in my path and speaks to me too fast. His tone is mild, friendly even, but Nest whirls to face the graybeard with huge, startled eyes.

"H-he's wrong," she stammers, but in her panic she speaks in Welsh. "My husband will pay for us both."

The graybeard grabs her arm and marches her toward the rope ladder. Nest struggles, arguing in haphazard Norse-Irish, but he pays no mind. She swivels and cries, "Elen. Elen!"

I try to rush toward her, but the sailor blocks me — this way, that way — and his friendly smile takes on an edge of warning. Her protests turn plea as her windblown golden head disappears over the side, hand over hand down the ladder. The last thing I hear before the crush of water drowns her voice is *I'm sorry.*

Gerald of Windsor must have refused to pay my passage. After all I did for his children, for him to serve me this way. He deserves the vengeance Owain will visit on him, and that day cannot come soon enough.

Given half a chance, I might end him myself.

There's a scuffle and a splash. The rowboat glides across the harbor toward shore with a sailor at the oars and the graybeard and Nest at the bow. She's hooded now, her hands pressed to her face.

Rhys smiles, the bastard, smiles like he's won. He even lifts a cheerful hand to wave Nest on her way.

"Passage," the captain says to Rhys in his clunky Welsh, and the penteulu sailor appears with the open strongbox.

Rhys reaches beneath his cloak, then begins frantically patting his midsection. "My purse. It's gone. One of you stole my purse!"

"I've no idea what you're speaking of," the captain replies in a voice of honey. "You must have forgotten it. Why else would you demand I turn around?"

Rhys goes ashen. His hands fall still. "God rot you."

"What, no silver?" The captain smiles. "Then we'll get our price on the Dublin slave docks."

Rhys darts a glance toward the side of the ship, and that's when they seize him. He struggles and bawls, "God damn every last man of you thieves!"

A heavy presence appears at my elbow. It's the captain, and he leans tree-bough arms against the rail and squints at the harbor. It takes all my will, but I keep from shrinking from him, even though big Norse-Irish sailors are binding Rhys's wrists and I am very, very afraid.

"Now then," the captain says, "about your passage."

"G-Gerald of Windsor should have paid you."

"He did not know you. He had not even heard your name."

I lick my lips. "His wife. She arranged it."

"The Englishman barely had the silver to pay her way," the captain replies. "Once the price went up."

Once the price went up. Gerald of Windsor didn't betray me.

"So now you owe me for your passage." The captain speaks to the harbor, his posture easy. He has no need to corner me. This is a ship thirty paces long. I've nowhere to go. "Or it'll be the slave docks for you as well."

"I can pay." I pull Owain's purse from where it hangs beneath my armpit. I grip it hard so there's no trembling. "Part now, and part when I'm on shore."

The captain holds out a weathered brown hand, and I fill it with silver. As I pour, I sneak glances at the wharves. A number of horses cluster nearby, spilling down the rickety waterside lane. That's them. Gerald of Windsor is collecting Nest right now. She'll be telling him there's been a mistake. That somehow he must put together coin enough to get me off this ship.

The rowboat is back, and the sailor appears on deck. The captain tilts my coins, nods, and gestures to the ladder.

Rhys writhes and curses while sailors tether him to the mast. One slams a meaty fist into his jaw, and he slumps against the ropes. His warband hardness is gone, and he's all boy now, bone-scared and greensick.

Mayhap this is what Einion ap Tewdwr saw when he shoved them clear of me one by one. All hardness gone. Empty hands.

"Him too." I drag my eyes away from the wharves and point at Rhys. "I'll cover his passage. Let him go."

The captain laughs. "Your silver pays for you. Now get in the boat before I change my mind."

"I'll give you a ring for him."

"Let's see it."

I fling my rucksack off my shoulder, reach down to the bottom, and pull out Owain's heavy gold ring. I'm cold, down to my vitals, and I can't stop shaking.

The captain takes the ring with one hand, and with the other jerks my rucksack out of my grip and scatters the contents across the deck. Owain's dagger and the silver torc for Cadwgan and the bracelets and necklets Owain's given me over the years and every stitch of clothing not this moment on my back—all of it flies over the planks for God and man to see.

"The lot will satisfy me, honeycomb," the captain says as the penteulu sailor collects the valuables into the strongbox. "Hope he's worth it."

The sailors cut the ropes and shove Rhys toward me. He comes rubbing both wrists, pulling in deep shuddery breaths, and tries to shake hair over his eyes that isn't there anymore, so all he can do is shove past me toward the ladder. I'm right behind him. I don't even pick up my clothes. I fumble blindly down slippery hempen rungs as fast as I dare and try not to think on the view I must be giving the oarsman as my skirts bell out in the sharp breeze.

The moment my backside hits the makeshift seat, I cry, "Go! Hurry!"

The oarsman glances at Rhys crouching sullenly in the bow, then up at his captain, who waves us clear. He grins at me, up and down and winky, then pushes off the cog with one dripping oar, turns us, and rows through the choppy harbor.

Up on deck I could see the wharves and horses fine, but down here it's just a wash of color, even if I half rise from my seat and peer hard across the glittering bay. Someone is sure to know where they've taken lodging. Perhaps Gerald left a man on the wharf to meet me in case I worked out a way to get off the ship myself.

I'm still trembling. Still cold.

The rowboat pulls up to a wharf chockablock with sailors calling to one another in a dozen languages. There are men with skin that's brown like rich mahogany, and men whose pale faces have burned a peeling red. Nest is nowhere in sight. Neither is Gerald of Windsor. Not a single horse or waiting retainer. Just a chaos of torn mud and manure.

Rhys is first out of the rowboat and halfway up the wharf before it's even tethered. I climb onto the planks after him, hand the second half of the passage money to the oarsman, then ask, "The other girl. This wharf?"

"Her man had horses waiting in the road." The sailor holds his hands like reins galloping, then points away at the distant hills.

Of course Gerald of Windsor would not want to spend one moment outside of sturdy walls once he got his wife back. He might have even suspected treachery after being fleeced by the graybeard, or the captain, or both. I blink back tears as I thank the oarsman. He nods, waves, and rows back toward the cog while I lean against a damp post and shiver.

Rhys is pacing. Talking to himself in a low mutter. "This is bad. It'll be se'ennights till she's back with Owain. No passage money. Nothing to trade."

Not moments ago, we both nearly landed on the Dublin slave docks. Now Rhys is on about hauling me back to Owain as if nothing happened. He could at least *thank* me for what I did. Knowing what it cost. Knowing what would have happened had I done nothing.

"My lord Cadwgan. I'll beg some coin of him. There's nothing else to do, and he may not like it. It has to work, though. Please let it work."

One side of Rhys's face is screaming red, and his eye will be purple by morning. His cloak is firmly cinched, and not just against the wind.

Oh. I know what this is. These are echoes talking. This is Rhys fighting ghosts of the unspeakable, trying to make things ordinary. He stood alone. No armed brothers with him who would have stepped up with drawn steel, odds be damned. Just a girl who had every reason to stand by and let the sailors finish their work.

I know something of that. I may not be in Owain's teulu, but I have looked unspeakable right in the eye.

Rhys is rubbing his thumbnail. The same motion as praying with a paternoster had it not been taken off him by the sailors. "Saint Elen is looking to Owain. She must be. Nothing less would keep the Normans from taking her. For making it so I could bring her back to him."

I close my eyes.

"You never said it." Rhys has fallen still. Arms crossed over his belly. Blocking the road.

He's not looking at me, but I know he wants an answer, so I reply, "Never said what?"

"That you left of your own choosing. *She* said you did." Rhys peers at me hopefully, head tilted as if he still had stringy curls to hide behind. "Did you?"

I cannot outrun Rhys. I can't overpower him. I definitely can't convince him to help me find Nest.

At a royal residence, I'll be safe while I catch my breath. Owain is forbidden to come home till Cadwgan sends for him. That could be tomorrow. It could be two years from now. The last we heard, Madog ap Rhirid held all of what was once Cadwgan's with the blessing of the English king, and Cadwgan was in the wind pulling strings and calling in favors. Owain still has a price on his head that the English king would very much like to redeem. Owain coming back, reminding everyone why this happened at all, would only make things worse.

"Can we just walk? Away from here?" I gesture at the path leading out of the village. "Please?"

"You must stay close. I promised I'd find you. Keep you safe." Rhys keeps rubbing his thumbnail. "Owain needs you with him. He's got enough to worry about. He heard that his kinsmen who backed Madog ap Rhirid's invasion did it because Cadwgan paid them to. That Cadwgan wanted to teach Owain a lesson, to force him to give Nest back and make him cool his heels in exile. Make him more obedient. Humble him."

That story has the sound of someone stirring the pot. It can't be true. Cadwgan ap Bleddyn would never take such a risk with his kingdom. But whether it's true won't matter if it's what Owain believes.

"I'll not run away." I'm not sure I can. Not shivering like I am.

"Good. We must hurry."

It hadn't been quite a threemonth the first time I thought to flee Owain ap Cadwgan. I wasn't running anywhere, though. Just *away*. So when Einion ap Tewdwr broke me with that single line and brought me back, at least I was going *somewhere*.

This time, I will think it through. This time, I will have a plan.

JuLy 1110

SOMETHING IS STRANGE ABOUT THE FORT RHYS leads me toward. It seems ordinary enough — sturdy wooden wall, set on a hill — but it's completely unspoiled. There are no piles of burned timber. No scaffolding holding up new buildings. Then sentries call to us in French, and of a sudden I realize why I don't recognize this fort and where we must be. Powys is in the hands of Madog ap Rhirid, who chased Owain over the sea, and Heaven only knows what's befallen Ceredigion. This must be the land on the border with England that Isabel brought Cadwgan in marriage.

Quite possibly the only land still held by the house of Bleddyn. Little wonder Rhys made his way directly here.

Rhys speaks French surprisingly well, and we're soon through the gate. He plows straight toward the hall, but a happy baby squeal brings my head around like a string toy. A matronly woman is holding little Henry ap Cadwgan on her hip near the rain barrel. She's dressed for traveling and has a rucksack over her shoulder. For the longest moment, I'm taken by how big Henry has gotten. I'm still looking for the unsteady little boy clinging to his nurse's forefingers at Aberaeron. He's leaner and taller, and someone trimmed away the baby curls that once trailed down his neck. Two warbanders pause to speak with Henry's nurse, then they fall into step beside her, and the four of them leave the fort.

". . . from Ireland," Cadwgan is saying as he steps out of the hall, Rhys at his heels like a puppy. "Madog took the bait. I don't think he even realized his *allies* were keeping him on a leash. He had his fun playing king, but time has come for boys to go home and men to step into the field."

"Your son will be glad to hear it, my lord." Rhys can't hide his grin. "He's been champing at the bit to come home since he set foot there."

"Take a meal and collect yourself, then be on board whatever next sails with the tide," Cadwgan says. "Tell Owain to go directly to Powys. My steward at Llyssun will be expecting him."

I can't breathe. Owain's coming home. It's not enough time. I'm not ready.

"You don't want him to present himself before you?" Rhys asks.

"I'm to have no contact with my errant son. According to the English king, it's a condition of his gracious recognition that what's mine is actually mine." When Cadwgan's voice goes mocking like that, it's eerie how much he sounds like Owain.

Rhys nods slowly. "We hadn't heard you'd come to terms

with the English king. Only that Madog was struggling to hold Powys and Ceredigion in a way that satisfied him."

"Madog promised peaceful governance. There's no kind of peace in either of those places. That kind of peace takes a king, and Madog is not a king." Cadwgan smiles faintly. "Henry of the English has lost patience with him and agreed to restore to me my lands—as if they're his to grant—if I cough up a bribe and hand over a hostage and swear to cut ties with Owain."

"You're not really, are you?" Rhys looks alarmed.

Cadwgan scoffs. "Lad, my son can be a blowhard wantwit, but he's my son, and if I cut him off, it won't be because the English king demands it of me. So Owain is not returning from Ireland because I bid him. He's coming back because his feckless cousin plundered a kingdom that will one day be his, and taking it from Madog means he will have a birthright once more. For no reason should Owain come to Ceredigion or so much as send a runner to me there till this all dies down." He lifts his brows. "Is that clear?"

"It is, my lord."

I grip the nearest wall. Owain will be in Powys soon. I thought to have more time. Earn some coin. Steal some food. Anything that would help me get to Nest and the little ones.

"Is Nest still with him?" Cadwgan growls.

"No. She's back with her husband."

"That's something, at least," he says with a sigh. "Not that it'll help me smooth things over, but at least my blowhard wantwit son isn't making it worse."

Inside the hall, a girl starts screaming, then there's the crash of things falling to the floor. I slide behind the corner of the stable, and Rhys fumbles for a sword long since taken off him, but Cadwgan muffles a groan. Isabel de Say appears at the door. Her veil is slipping and her scowl is murderous. She stalks outside like a beast on the hunt, muttering, "Where is he, where's the son of a—there you are! I'll kill you with my bare hands, you filthy excuse for a man!"

She flies at Cadwgan, but he catches her wrists and holds them to her sides firmly yet without violence. Her mouth is free, though, and she pours abuse on him in three languages that would impress even the lads of Owain's warband. If Isabel is suffering, I'm not exactly sorry for it, but I've called Cadwgan those names in my head enough times that someone shouting them makes me smile.

"Sweeting, you knew it was coming," Cadwgan says. "I thought it would be easier this way."

"Easier?" Isabel struggles free and stomps away several paces. "You're a bigger bastard than I reckoned if you thought as much. All that silver wasn't enough. You gave my little Henry as a hostage to the king and sent him away all thief-in-the-night so I couldn't even say farewell. That's easier than *what*?"

I stop smiling. At least she didn't have to listen to wailing getting fainter, but she also didn't get a chance to tell him she'd be back.

"*Our* little Henry," Cadwgan replies patiently. "A hostage was part of the terms. It's why we can return to Ceredigion now."

"You have other sons. Why Henry?"

"I'm married to *you*. The English set a lot of store by such things. They'd not consider one of my other sons as valuable." Cadwgan raises an eyebrow. "Besides, why do you think I didn't object to naming him Henry?"

Isabel hisses.

"No harm will come to him. Henry's got his nurse and that whipping top he loves. He's going to the royal court of England, for Christ's sake. He's in more danger here than there! And if all goes well, he could be back by next summer. That's hardly any time at all."

"Ugh, I cannot even stand to look at you!"

"Sweeting, be reas—"

But she's gone, turned on her heel and stomping toward the stable while wrenching her veil over her ears. I crouch farther around the corner as Isabel moves through the doorway, muttering a low stream of bad words in French. At the hall door, Cadwgan hands Rhys a purse, aims him toward the kitchen, then disappears inside.

The moment Cadwgan is gone, Isabel storms out of the stable, towing a horse by the bridle. She bellows a name, and a burly warbander rises wearily from an upturned bucket. Still cursing, Isabel flings the reins at the warbander and tries to haul herself onto the horse's back without the mounting block.

"We're leaving?" the warbander asks. "What about your things, my lady?"

"I have everything I need at Worthen," Isabel snaps. "Hurry

up. Let's see how that filthy wretch likes someone leaving without the benefit of a farewell."

I haven't had a decent meal since Ireland. My last mouthful of travel bread was yesterday night, and my feet haven't blister-keened this much since fleeing ahead of Madog ap Rhirid's warband all those months ago. Now that Rhys has passage money, we'll be on our way to the coast this very day. I'll be standing before Owain, who I robbed and left saintless, before a fortnight is out.

Isabel is growling away from Cadwgan instead of feasting in the hall at his right hand. If Nest could bring herself to trust me, I must take a chance on Isabel de Say. I step into the yard and call, "My lady, wait!"

A flicker of disgust passes over her face, but it's fleeting, like she doesn't even have the will to hate me. "What? What do you want?"

Isabel looks hagridden, cheeks flushed and plaits tatty beneath her hood. She is nowhere near the girl with the jewel-blue eyes and cold hands who dislodged Cadwgan's grip from my arm at Aberaeron.

"I heard," I reply quietly. "About Henry. I'm sorry. It was a right bastard thing for Cadwgan to do. You must be wrecked."

"What do you know of it?"

I cough a bitter laugh. "If you're looking for a way to get back at him, I've got one."

In an instant she's attentive, like a dog when you show it meat.

"You're going to your hunting lodge, are you not? Worthen? Let me come with you as your guest. Once Cadwgan learns of it, he'll be wroth as ten baited bears, but there'll be nothing he can do. Not when you're at Worthen."

Isabel squints at me. I hold my breath. Sway on my feet.

Then she smiles, hard and catlike. "Yes. He wants you nowhere near me. He'd hate it. So by all means yes. You are most welcome."

Worthen this time of year will be filling up with new onions and leeks from the garden and big round cheeses and likely some mutton. Isabel can't watch my every move. I'll pass a day there. Perhaps two. When she no longer finds it amusing to have me around, I will be rested and healthy. I'll raid her larder and head straight for Dyfed where Nest and the little ones are waiting.

"May I say farewell?" I gesture at Rhys standing in the shadow of the hall door, poking through a shine of silver in his palm.

Isabel nods absently as she fusses with a bulky parcel that a servant is strapping behind her saddle. As I near, Rhys is miserably dragging a finger through the coins.

"It's not enough for us both," he murmurs.

Betimes Rhys is a warbander, lean and fierce and capable. Other times he's a wide-eyed boy of four and ten. "Cadwgan means for you to go alone. I'm to go to Worthen with Isabel. I'll be safer there. Away from all those sailors."

Rhys shudders. He glances at Isabel and her burly warbander. He bites his lip.

"Saint Elen looks to Owain," I go on softly. "Why else would Isabel of all people invite me into her home?"

"Very well." Rhys closes a fist around the silver and tight-wraps it into the purse. "Please be careful. Owain can't lose you."

I nod. Rhys hovers a hand to clap me on the back warband-style, but ducks his head and follows the steward who's been standing by. The steward speaks of ale and bread as he leads Rhys inside.

Isabel is waiting by the gate, glancing impatiently at the hall door every other moment. We're soon into a greenwood full of birdsong and wind-rustle and fresh dewy undergrowth. I'm not fooled, though. Terms or not, chances are good there are still warbands on the prowl who'd love to put their hands on any-thing worth something to Owain ap Cadwgan.

I'll ask at steadings till I fumble my way to Dyfed. From there, finding Nest should be as simple as pleading an audience at the first thing with a high, sturdy wall. I'll beg what I can and steal what I have to. By the time Owain's in Wales once more, I'll be in a place he'll want to think twice and thrice about raiding to get me back.

Besides, he'll have a kingdom to retake.

I close my eyes and think to pray to Saint Elen, but instead I'm whispering my promise aloud to the birds and sunshine, to the little ones wherever they are.

I'll come back. I'll always come back.

†

ORDINARY LADIES WOULD SIT THEMSELVES ON THE
hearth bench when they got home, or ask for a mug of ale,
or change into clean clothes, or hug a favorite servant or pet a
joyful dog.

Isabel orders the linens stripped off the bed and burned.

She stands before the gathered servants with her boots still
muddy from the journey, two steps past Worthen's threshold and
stabbing her finger at them like a firebrand. The servants trade
wide-eyed looks. As two of them edge toward the bed, Isabel
demands that every last thing Cadwgan might have touched
be scrubbed with lye, from the armrests of the big chair at the
high table down to the supper spoons. She hollers at the steward
when he refuses to burn the linens, and she's only barely swayed
by the argument that it's the only set in the house.

Worthen is Isabel's, part of her dower share. Owain explained the Norman custom to me once while telling me he didn't want his hellcat stepmother's patch of border dirt anyway. When Cadwgan dies, Worthen will not pass with the rest of his lands to his sons. It will always belong to Isabel. It was her father's, and now it's hers and only hers.

"Very well. Fine. But scrub those linens with lye like the rest." Isabel drags a wrist over her eyes. "I don't care if they won't be dry by sundown! I'd rather sleep on the floor! And I want to know if he dares set foot in the courtyard."

The steward looks pained, but mumbles, "Yes, m'lady," and departs.

"I'll burn *something* of his," Isabel mutters. "Come."

She drags me across the hall to a curtained alcove. Servants are carrying away the linens and piling the bedclothes on a rack for airing. Isabel marches to a coffer and swears when she can't pry the lock. She kicks it and staggers back clutching her toe, cursing like a dockside ganger. Then she slumps on her heels, wiping her eyes, trembling.

That first year, I was never far from vengeance. I thought of the knife nearly every day. I could do it. It wasn't like I'd never killed a man.

"What else does he love?" I ask. "That's not locked up?"

Isabel shields her face with her elbow. "Don't look at me."

"I'm not." Seeing Isabel weeping and thwarted should make me smile, but she's alone here in this place that's only hers. "I'm asking what Cadwgan loves that you can get to. So you can ruin that instead."

She snorts. "His warband. His dogs. His sword."

In Ireland I spent months playacting as Owain's wife. I wore undergarments and shoes and spun with the daughter of the house and sat at Owain's right hand and delighted in how ordinary it felt. Before me is Isabel de Say, the wife of Cadwgan ap Bleddyn, who is king of Powys and lord of Ceredigion. Her place secure, for all the good it does her. She is not just any wife, and even her child isn't safe. There are locked chests in this house that should be hers alone.

It would be no different for any proper wife of Owain ap Cadwgan.

"His wine." Isabel's head bobs up. "There was a cask of claret left over from when His Grace King Henry was here. The *good* wine that costs a fortune. You-know-who says he's saving it for the next time he has to eat crow before an enemy. It's hidden in the kitchen."

I nod. It'll gush like a bleeding wound and make purple mud in the courtyard.

"We're going to roll that barrel into the hall." Isabel sits up straighter and grins. It's the same smile she aimed at me at Aberaeron, but this time it seems cozy and sly, like Margred planning a birthday surprise. "We'll drink every drop."

The steward protests, then forbids. Isabel elbows past him with two mugs and taps the cask herself with a meat knife. She fills them, then stations a big kettle beneath the burbling leak. One mug she shoves at me. The other she takes a big drink from while the steward goes twitchy and his color rises.

"I've got witnesses," he mutters, and all but flies away. Isabel giggles and takes another drink, and she gives me such a look that I cautiously do the same. The wine is undiluted, and I nearly sputter. I've just drunk the cost of a whole summer's worth of some poor man's labor in one swallow.

Isabel pulls me toward the big bed in the corner, now stripped down to the fat straw-stuffed pallet that perches upon zigs and zags of tightly strung hemp. She climbs up and looks at me expectantly.

I hesitate. I'm here to *steal*, not comb Isabel's hair and gossip.

The bed whispers promises. Every muscle in my body keens. Ireland feels years away, and I can barely remember the last time I slept well. Passing one night in some kind of comfort will not undo my plan. Besides, it will be easier to pilfer if Isabel trusts me and does not suspect till it's too late.

I climb up after her. Isabel pulls the curtains closed, and we're plunged into a gauzy darkness. It would be like the maidens' quarters if I trusted her at all. She slides till her back is against the wall, holding her mug aloft to keep from sloshing. I fold my legs and take a small drink. It's like the high king's wine. Strong and rich, so good there's no grit on your teeth.

"Do you think you-know-who has worked it out by now?"

Isabel takes a hearty swig. "That you left with me? That you're my guest?"

I shrug. I don't tell her that Cadwgan likely had no idea I'd come with Rhys. Cadwgan has been looking for a way to be rid of me since the first time Owain put an arm around my waist and explained why I was holding his elbow and would be needing a place at table. Had Cadwgan seen me in the courtyard, Owain far away in Ireland, I doubt I'd have left that border fort alive.

"Likely he's more worried about Powys and Owain returning and what Madog will do once he learns of the English king's terms." At her scowl, I hurry to add, "But don't worry. Your husband will be good and angry when he does finally learn of it."

"Owain ap Cadwgan." Isabel spits it like a curse and takes another long drink. "I'd like to slap him senseless. Had he just gone to war, none of this would have happened and Henry would still be with me."

She peers at me like I'll defend him. Like she *wants* me to so she can go on at length what a bastard he is. But I know something of vengeance, and if you let it move through you and keep it from settling in your quietest places, over time it will trickle away. There is nothing to defend here. Owain did not have to abduct Nest, much less the little ones. He could have sent them back when his father bid him. He definitely did not have to humiliate her again and again and make them all suffer at every chance. Another man might have made vengeance a weapon, sharp and hungry, and gathered a warband about him, but

Owain ap Cadwgan was not content with ordinary vengeance. His was a vengeance to preside over. One that would make allies and enemies alike as wary of crossing him as they were his father.

I drain half the mug and let it burn all the way down.

"I wager a whole shilling that Owain did all this on purpose," Isabel says. "He'd have my son stay a hostage forever."

Llywelyn penteulu, his neck open to the sky. His harsh, shallow gasping. Owain biting his knuckles, touching the scar beneath his arm like it burned.

"It's got nothing to do with your baby." I upend my mug again.

The world is beginning to blur at the edges, and my whole body feels full of honeybees calmly lulling with warm flowers and gentle buzzing. It's getting easier not to think about Owain. To let the bees drown him out.

Isabel's lip trembles. "Henry still smells like milk. He can say *Mama* now. He has such tiny little feet, and you should see the way he rushes over squealing when he sees me . . ."

Her voice gets quiet and sweet and loses those sharp Norman angles and her hair gets darker and she becomes Rhael. Rhael who once snuggled next to me on our pallet in the steading, where we'd whisper about whether lambs could be taught to count and whose hair was shinier and if there'd be ginger cake for May Eve again this year.

"Owain saw an opportunity." I won't think how Nest limped into the courtyard that first day barefoot and in her nightgown. "The rest of it? Madog ap Rhirid invading Powys because he was lured by Gerald's bounty? All those kinsmen who backed him? That was a gut-punch."

Rhael snickers and she becomes Isabel again, and I down another fierce swallow of wine because mayhap it'll bring my sister back, even for a moment.

"My fool husband got those men to help Madog," Isabel says over the rim of her mug. "It's not like that came cheap, either."

I choke on my wine. "It's *true*? Cadwgan ap Bleddyn paid his own kinsmen to support Madog's invasion? But Madog holds Powys now while Cadwgan is holed up on your lands!"

"Yes. But no. Madog held Powys and Ceredigion because he was permitted to. You-know-who let it happen and convinced his kinsmen to keep Madog from making too big a mess of it. Now Madog is a breath from losing both. He promised His Grace the king that there would be peace and law. Instead every vale is crawling with warbands." Isabel giggles and pokes me with her toe. "Can't *imagine* who might be behind such disorder. Can you?"

I take another long, steadying drink. "So Cadwgan allows Owain to return from Ireland. Now that he's made sure Powys is reeling and helpless, and Owain spoiling to reclaim it after stewing for months in exile. That bastard doesn't even have to get his hands dirty."

"My husband may be a fool *and* a bastard," Isabel says, tipping her mug, "but he knows well that retaking Powys from the likes of Madog ap Rhirid will be easier by tenscore than it would from Gerald of Windsor or Gilbert fitz Richard de Clare. Madog holding Powys and Ceredigion—and His Grace the king giving his blessing—meant no Norman lord could simply invade."

I finish my wine in one bitter swallow. Rhys was right, and Owain was right to believe it. Cadwgan has been pulling strings this whole time to make all the puppets dance, and he comes out of it getting everything he wants. His kingdom and province back. His Norman enemies denied a foothold anywhere in his lands. The English king foiled and befuddled.

His son broken to bridle, brought to heel.

"Cadwgan ap Bleddyn had better live forever," I say quietly, "for none of his schemes will survive him."

"Can I ask you something?" says Rhael.

I'm lying on my back, my hair loose from its pins and streaming every which way. My half-full mug dangles from my fingers over the edge of the bed. I've lost count how many I've had. "All right."

"What are you doing here?"

I roll my head so I'm lying on my ear. Rhael sprawls beside me. She looks nothing like herself, but I'm beyond caring. "I'm here 'cause you invited me."

"No. No. I mean, what are you doing here when Owain isn't here? Don't you do that . . . saint thing . . . for him?"

I'm about to say something I know I shouldn't, but I have to say it because Rhael always knows when I lie. Even as the words are happening, I wish I could have them back, but I am full of honeybees, warm and dizzy and liquid inside. "I'm here when he isn't because I won't be seeing him again."

Rhael frowns, and Isabel starts to shade through till I close my eyes to keep my sister here.

"But . . . he's coming back from Ireland, isn't he?"

"I won't be here. I'll be in Dyfed."

"Why?" She's definitely Isabel now, whether my eyes are open or not.

I hoist myself up and empty my mug. "Nest's little ones love me. I will be their nurse. Not their pet."

"What about Owain? Won't he want his saint back? Won't he *need* her back?"

"What *about* him?" I roll the purple dregs across the pewter mug bottom. My whole belly is sour and churny. "What do you care, anyway? Didn't you just say that he did all this on purpose so the Normans would take baby Henry and roast him on a spit when Cadwgan puts one foot out of line? And I do mean *when.* Not *if.*"

Isabel hardens. All of her. Shoulders. Jaw. Eyes. She holds out an insistent hand for my empty mug. "More wine. Whatever we can't drink, we'll give to the pigs."

I'm dead. That's what this is.

Only the dead don't need to piss.

I'm sprawled crosswise over a bed, fully dressed. My mouth is sawdust, and I'll heave my guts if I move anything, and yet

I'll be worse than dead if I piss a bed belonging to the king of Powys. So I slide off one side. Crunch onto my knees. Reach around, forehead pressed to the side of the pallet, until I find a bowl. For a brief moment I'm glad for the bedcurtains, but I've pissed behind my cloak on the decks of merchant ships while a dozen Norse-Irish sailors muttered at my turned back like I was a mystery play. Worthen might as well be a chapel.

Isabel is retching on the floor, hanging her head over the other side of the bed. When she's done, she curls up on the bare pallet like a dead insect and grinds the heels of her hands into her eyes. I leave the bowlful of piss on the floor and crawl back onto the bed beside her. Because my head. Is throbbing. Like an anvil. And I. Am dying.

If I'm dead, it won't matter if I sleep.

It's later when I peel my eyes open to a wool-scratchy tongue and a tiny piercing pain deep behind my forehead. The sun's in a different place, slanting through the open front door. There's a flagon of small ale by the bed, and I'm so thirsty I down every drop without taking a breath. Beside me, Isabel winces as she stretches. She doesn't look nearly as wrung out as I feel. Mayhap this is not the first time she's had so much wine at once.

"It was foolish of me to make them wash the linens." Isabel grins at me, sly and mischievous. "That was possibly the worst night's sleep I've ever had. I blame you-know-who. The bastard."

I'm struggling for words, and the swimmy fog in my head doesn't help. Servants are setting up the trestle table for breakfast, and Isabel rolls off the bed and pulls me toward them. There's bread that's been toasted, and porridge, and lots more small ale.

"How were we not friends before?" Isabel asks cheerfully between bites of porridge. "I should have known you-know-who was wrong about you. He's wrong about most everything else."

I smile and gesture at my full mouth as a reason I can't reply, but there's no malice to her. It's like she's forgotten Aberaeron ever happened. Like we've always been arm-link sisters, sharing wine and secrets in the dark. This means I can do one better than rob the house. My new friend is going to develop an overwhelming urge to send me to Dyfed and the little ones with a full rucksack and a guide. On Cadwgan's coin.

After breakfast, Isabel gives me two of her old gowns. She chatters about color and cut, then calls for a basin of water and pushes me toward the bedcurtains. I've got one eye on the door, though. For all Isabel's bold talk, if Cadwgan shows up here, they're not going to keep him out.

Behind the bedcurtains, I fumble with the basin and spill water on myself. I'm still a little blurry from the wine. The hall feels muffled in here, like it's under a blanket of snow. The shuffle of servants sweeping and tidying, the creak of the well windlass, the clatter of wood and crockery. I half expect to push apart the heavy woolen folds and greet Gormlaith and Aoife, to have servants nodding to me because I'm Owain's wife.

It's not always enough to know ordinary if you see it. Sometimes you must touch it to believe it's possible, and Owain's wife had that chance in Ireland. But this is Worthen, and I'm scheming a way to pull the wool over Isabel's eyes. I'm looking over both shoulders for Cadwgan. All the shoes and undershifts in the kingdoms of Wales can't make me something the house of Bleddyn will look at and not through.

Once I hoped Isabel could carve me out a place in this family. She can't, though. She never could and neither can I, because in truth, there is no place for me here.

Ordinary is waiting for me in Dyfed.

I find Isabel spinning in the dooryard on one of the hall benches. I join her in the birdsong and sunlight, and I snap off a long stem of grass. Somewhere to the south, William and David are playing ball. Not Miv may be taking her first steps, and I have not yet come back.

"I wonder how long till Owain returns," I muse.

"I hope he *never* returns. I hope his ship sinks and he dies in terror." Isabel peers at me sidelong. "It can now, yes? Since you're not with him?"

I want badly to turn my eyes Heavenward and beg Saint Elen that it not be from Isabel's lips to God's ears. Instead I toy with the stem and say, "If I'm in Dyfed looking after Nest's children, I'll never be near Owain again. Gerald of Windsor will make very certain of that. It's a long way from here, though. I'm not sure I know the way. Once Owain's back, he'll never let me out of his sight again."

Isabel jumbles her spinning in her lap. "What if I send one

of my swordsmen with you? Give you food for the journey? I can do that. You-know-who can't stop me."

An armed escort. That's even better than I hoped for. "My lady! That's so kind of you! I can be ready to leave right away."

"What, now?" Isabel makes a dismissive gesture and untangles her leader yarn. "Before you-know-who learns that you're here under my protection and there's nothing he can do about it? No, I want him to stew in that a while. Also, don't call me *my lady* when he's around. It'll irk him sorely to hear you call me Isabel."

"But Owain will be back soon!" Too panicky. I force my voice calm. "I doubt he'll go straight to Powys like he was told. He'll come get me first."

Isabel smiles, coy and playful. "Don't you worry. We'll be sure you're gone before he lands. Besides, I'm not afraid of Owain. My wolfhound is more clever."

It's only been a day. I'd planned to pass a short while here anyway. A little longer won't hurt, but knowing Nest and the children are waiting makes it hard to nod along.

Beside me, Isabel hums a little tune as she spins. She doesn't know Owain like I do. She has no idea what Saint Elen means to him, how deep down it goes, and what he'll do to get her protection back.

THE NEXT DAY IS FAIR, AND ISABEL WANTS TO GO FOR a walk along a deer path. She chatters about Henry and how much she misses him, but I can't keep from looking over my shoulder every other pace, listening for hooves at the approach.

"Cadwgan must have heard by now," I say, letting the idea hang between us, but Isabel scoffs and takes my hand and swings it.

"You worry too much. Come, just enjoy the day."

In one breath she misses her baby. In the next she's telling me to enjoy the day. Perhaps later she'll complain about bland stew, like worse things don't happen to the daughters of fallen kings and slain drovers alike.

The linens are finally dry, and Isabel has the servants make up the bed, so at least we have the prospect of a decent night's sleep. But I lie awake staring at the curtains and wondering whether Rhys has made it to the coast, whether he's already sailed with the tide, whether he's even made it out of Powys without being slain by someone's warband.

The days linger and crawl. My yarn is a mess. I tap my foot. I go to the privy every other moment, walking slow past the gate and straining my ears for footfalls.

Isabel frowns at me over her neat skeins. "That's very tiresome, you know. All your fidgeting."

"Then send me to Dyfed," I say, and it's all I can do to ask and not plead.

"It's hurtful, too. Like you can't wait to leave."

I flutter a smile. "Please forgive me. You've been most kind."

"I'll let you go soon, I promise. I'd have you-know-who truly squirm. Besides, we're having a nice time together, aren't we? We're all but kin, you know." Isabel smiles like she can't wait to say that in front of Cadwgan.

There was a time when I thought being close to Isabel would solve everything. If this kind of self-serving excuse for company and showy, false companionship is what proper wives can expect, Margred doesn't need toys. She needs holy orders.

The house of Bleddyn might never be ordinary. Mayhap it can't be. What Margred needs is somewhere she'll always be welcome. Someone to throw the door open and hug her hard, even when everyone else looks through her and past her. She's always done that much for me. Soon enough I can return that favor.

Tomorrow. First light. I am leaving Worthen even if it's with nothing but the clothes on my back. This time, I will get myself clear.

AT BREAKFAST, I EAT EVERYTHING IN SIGHT. NEST will lay out a feast in my honor when I reach Dyfed, but I must get there first. Across the table, Isabel tucks into porridge and natters on about Henry and doesn't notice me sneaking oatcakes into my lap and wrapping them in a stolen washrag. After breakfast, Isabel will corner the steward to discuss the day. It'll take her a while to find him, though, since he's usually passed out drunk in some odd place like the hayloft. After the business with the linens and the wine, I can hardly blame him for spending his days not quite sober and well out of her way.

That's when I'll go.

I'll slip my breakfast scavengings into my apron and tell the gateman I'm meeting Isabel for a ramble in the greenwood. He'll let me pass. I'll wander down the deer path, and when I'm out of sight, I'll run till I can't and then walk till it's dark. I know to go south and west. I'm rested, and I have small things to eat and a spare gown I can sell or trade.

I can do this.

Isabel rises from the table. "Well, I'm off to find that lay-about steward. Would you join me?"

"Try the storeroom. I think I saw him head that way." Calmly. Smile. "I'm going to sit outside a while. I want to embroider that gown you gave me. I'll bring out a bench."

"Good idea. I'll meet you there lat—" Isabel abruptly falls silent. Her face goes granite.

There in the doorway is Cadwgan ap Bleddyn, leaning on the frame.

I freeze like a sighted hare, but Isabel makes a graceful, ice-cold curtsy as she says, "My lord." Then she pulls me up from the bench, and I come staggering. Cadwgan's hangman gaze passes over me slow and heavy.

"May I?" he asks, gesturing to the threshold he has yet to step over.

Isabel narrows her eyes before finally nodding. Cadwgan crosses the hall toward her, but when she moves a pace away in a polite yet deliberate sidestep, he stops at the head of the table.

I should have left days ago. He'll wait till she's not looking. Then there'll be a "mischance."

Cadwgan clears his throat. He's not looking at me, though. Only Isabel. "Please tell me you know sending Henry as a hostage was the last thing I wanted to do."

Isabel folds her arms.

"Well, I hope at least you've had a chance to calm yourself. We're heading to Ceredigion on the morrow, so have your belongings together."

"There are things I must attend to first," she tells him coolly. "You could have given me some sort of warning. But I forgot who I stand before. You don't believe in giving warning, do you?"

Cadwgan sighs. "Sweeting, you are going to have to let this go."

Rhys appears in the doorway and shuffles. Cadwgan makes the *hold* gesture, two raised fingers, and he nods.

No. Rhys can't be back already. Something's not right.

Isabel turns to me. "You wanted to leave. You shall leave. I'll have my best swordsman take you wherever you want to go. Are you ready?"

"Oh saints, I most certainly —"

"No," Cadwgan cuts in. "This girl is not going anywhere."

Isabel looks ready to blacken his eye. "She'll go wherever she wants, and you won't stop her."

"She can go to hell for all I care," Cadwgan replies through his teeth, "but the one place she is *not* going is back to my son."

I swivel to face him. "I'm not going to Owain, my lord."

Cadwgan looks at me square for the first time since he walked in. "You — what?"

"I'm not going back to Owain." I repeat it clear and sure, even as Rhys behind him looks half raging and half bellysick.

"Where are you going, then?"

"She's going to Dyfed," Isabel puts in before I can spin out a convincing lie. "To be nurse to Gerald of Windsor's children."

Cadwgan was clearly expecting a different answer, for he draws back with a wide-eyed frown that takes him several long moments to master.

I press it, my only advantage. "We're of one mind, my lord. You'll never see me again."

"I'll take her." Rhys steps forward. "I'll see her safe to where she needs to be."

Cadwgan squints, first at me and then at Rhys. "Do you swear it? You may follow a warband led by my son, but this is your *king* you speak to."

"I swear it."

"My lord, don't send me with him." I grip my skirts with both hands. "He won't bring me to Nest. We'll go straight to Owain."

"I take a man at his word," Cadwgan replies. "Besides, Owain's still in Ireland. Even my son wouldn't be so great a fool as to defy me."

I gape at Rhys. "But you were going to fetch him!"

"He will," Cadwgan says, "now that I know where you are, and where you're going."

Rhys looks away, and I cough a quiet, bitter laugh at how deeply mistaken I was, thinking I could hide anything from Cadwgan ap Bleddyn.

"Don't blame this lad," Cadwgan goes on. "If it makes you feel any better, he tried hard to keep your whereabouts to himself. Hear me now, though. You have my leave to go to Nest. I owe her that much after what Owain did to her, and may you both know peace. But if I ever see you again, I will kill you myself, come what may. Saint Elen might protect my son. I can't expect to know the will of God Almighty, and Heaven knows it would explain a lot. You're the one whispering in his ear, though, and you sure as blazes aren't doing it for his benefit. So it ends now. It ends for good. Am I clear?"

If there was ever a time for Isabel to fly into a hellcat rage, to demand she have her way and shove me out the door behind a swordsman of her choosing, it's now.

But she's gone. Isabel de Say has left me here to burn.

I lift my chin. I look Cadwgan in the eye. "Very clear."

"Right then." Cadwgan hooks Rhys across the shoulders and pulls him several paces from me, mutters in his ear, then claps his back in a way I've seen Owain do a thousand times. It means that Rhys is dismissed and the matter is closed.

I'm trembling. Still clutching the spare gown Isabel gave me that I was going to pretend to embroider. I will walk out of Worthen alive, even after facing down a man who has waited years for a chance like this.

Cadwgan steps away toward the hearth, where Isabel is sulking. He doesn't wait for me to thank him. He doesn't care whether I'm grateful. He just wants me gone. Owain would have run me through where I stand.

All at once I wonder how Owain will ever be a king.

I'm carrying a wineskin filled with small ale, and bundled beneath my arm is meat and cheese wrapped in my spare gown.

It's been quiet too long, so I clear my throat and say, "So. Ah. How much further to Dyfed, do you reckon?"

Rhys holds back a tree limb so I can pass, then moves so we walk side by side.

"At least there'll be silver in it for you," I say into the silence. "Handfuls and handfuls. A fine horse, mayhap. I know you have no liking for this, but when you stand before Owain, you can tell him his father bade you. Your *king* gave you no choice."

Rhys grunts, but whether he's agreeing or simply responding I can't tell.

I check the sky once more to be sure we're heading southwest toward Dyfed and not north to Powys. "You shouldn't feel foolish. That Cadwgan worked out I'd come with you. That he got you to tell him I was at Worthen. I'm not upset. Honestly."

"I don't feel foolish. Whether I have any liking for this doesn't matter. I've been given a task, and I'm going to see it through."

The sun's still in the right place. We're going south and west. Whatever he promised Owain, whatever Owain promised *him,* Rhys is carrying out this task because it takes a rare man to look Cadwgan ap Bleddyn in the face and lie. A rarer man to defy him openly. Rhys is not that man.

When he was beaten into Owain's teulu last autumn, Rhys and I stood at eye level. Now I barely come up to his shoulder. He's broader now and his voice deeper, like a half-dug well. In another year he'll be someone else. A fighting man I'd hardly recognize.

Today, though, we're walking at elbows toward Dyfed, and every now and then he carelessly runs a thumb down his forearm. For today, he is still Rhys.

Pull back this branch. Not much longer and William will run at me squealing. Move past that stone. Nest will hug me, and I will hold out my arms for the baby.

Step into a clearing, and a dozen fighting men crouch around a cold meal. I scrabble for a fire iron I don't have, and one of them stands and it's Morgan. Morgan from Owain's warband. There's Llywarch and Gwilym and —

"Give her something to eat, will you?" Rhys says to them. "I can likely still catch a ship today if I keep moving."

"Don't bother," Morgan replies. "He's already here."

Morgan tips his head toward a stand of brush and my mouth falls open, but Rhys merely huffs a sigh, mutters something like *of course he is,* and gestures for me to follow.

I edge a step back. "Owain's in Ireland! Cadwgan said you'd not yet gone to fetch him!"

"I never said Owain wouldn't come back of his own choosing."

"You told Cadwgan —"

"I told my king I'd return you where you needed to be. That's what I'm doing. You need to be with Owain, and now you are."

I've been given a task and I'm going to see it through. Only not the one Cadwgan gave him.

Owain must have told Rhys where the warband would

assemble, and Rhys had the wit to turn up in this place before boarding a ship just in case. Or—saints, mayhap Owain hinted it would be wise for him to do just that.

I fall still. I cannot be here. There's no place for me. "Rhys, please don't do this. You heard Cadwgan. He will end me if I stay with Owain. Nest will reward you. Whatever you want. She'll give it to you."

"That's for Owain and his lord father to sort out." Rhys glares at me. "How can you still believe I'd betray Owain for thirty pieces of Norman silver?"

I'm counting days now. If Owain's here, he must have sailed from Ireland soon after we did. Long before his father gave him leave to do it. Nest and me escaping must have given Owain all the excuse he needed.

The brush shifts and Owain appears, blade in hand. Blade in hand in his own camp. He peers at me like he's not sure I'm real. He's somehow put his hands on new leather armor, and there's a grubby band of cloth tied around his upper arm.

Rhys is saying something about his task. Bowing his head. Owain wordlessly spins the dagger front to back, front to back.

I force my eyes off the blade. I draw a deep, shaky breath and say the only true thing in my head. "I'm glad to see you safe, my lord."

"Oh, aye," drawls Einion penteulu as he stations himself at Owain's elbow. "You wanted so much to see to his safety that you robbed him and abandoned him in a foreign kingdom."

Owain's face goes hard and he regrips his knife.

"That . . ." I can't pull in a whole breath. "Saint Elen, she . . ."

Einion penteulu smiles. "Seems to me that Owain spent all this time untouched without you. Mayhap Saint Elen will look to him anyway."

When Owain pets the smudgy cloth above his elbow, it flutters enough that I recognize the edging of embroidery. It's a strip of linen torn from a shift I left drying on an Irish clothesline. He's turned my undergarments into a relic of me, like I'm a saint, too.

"The boy did as you told him," Einion penteulu says to Owain in a smooth, treacherous voice, "but things have changed. He couldn't know. I'll attend to it, my lord."

Rhys is still standing next to me, but in two clean, sharp motions, Einion shoves him clear and swivels me away from Owain. Morgan steps closer, then Llywarch. One by one they gather, the lads of Owain's teulu, quiet and hulking like dogs waiting to set to.

"What the hell is this?" Rhys comes after us, but Einion, still smiling, pushes him hard at Gwilym, who holds him fast.

"Einion." I struggle to pry his fingers loose because I am against the steading wall and Rhael isn't here and I am very, very afraid. "This isn't what you think. If you'd just—"

"It's exactly what I think. Shut up or I'll shut you up." Einion penteulu hands me off to Morgan and Llywarch. They haul me fighting and stumbling toward the tree line while Einion slings an arm over Owain's shoulder, turns him bodily, and gestures to this tree and that hill while Owain fidgets with his charm, not putting a stop to this because Einion's voice has been the only one in his ear for way too long.

Rhys is shouting, cursing like a drover and begging the others to heed him, but Gwilym is built like a boar and twice as strong. He'll hold Rhys fast till this is over.

"You don't want this." I'm struggling now. Wrenching hard to catch Owain's eye. "Saint Elen — you want — Owain!"

"Oh yes." Einion cackles. "Keep telling a king's son what he wants."

"Don't you listen to him." My voice is raw. "Don't you listen to the Adversary. Not when you can listen to her."

Morgan shoves me against a tree hard enough to clatter my teeth. I brace for the ground, sobbing already, but something seizes my jaw and I force my eyes open and it's Owain. I haven't been this close to him in se'ennights, and I'm overwhelmed by the smell of him, the restless vigor that all but pours off him in waves.

"What was that?" he whispers.

"Be careful." I'm trembling. Cold to the marrow. If someone's going to end me here in the woods, by Christ may it be Owain ap Cadwgan and not one of these bastards. "Be careful who you listen to. Not everyone means you well."

Einion groans. "My lord, really. She must think you're a fool."

Owain nudges Morgan, and suddenly I'm free. Somehow I stay on my feet before Owain ap Cadwgan, who's worrying his charm like beads on a paternoster, with Einion penteulu hovering behind him, outraged and murderous. He is utterly still, not even a scowl or an eyebrow that I could reckon with. At length he whispers, "Say it again. Loud. So my penteulu can hear you."

I lick my lips. "Wh-what?"

"That I can *listen* to her." Owain's voice carries through the clearing, and Einion's jaw twitches although he stays silent.

The tree bark digs into my back. I pull in long, whistling breaths and let each one out as a silent curse on Rhys's head. All he had to do was see me safe to Dyfed. All he had to do was heed his king.

"For months I was trapped in exile, and my father was the one who kept me there. I might have forgiven that. Someday." Owain leans close, fast and smooth like a striking snake, and I flinch like I haven't in years. "But he's in league with Gerald of Windsor now. I know he is. It's why he sent some bastard to kidnap you and Nest. Stole you both right out from under me just so he would have his way and I'd have nothing. Like he wants. Like he's *always* wanted."

It's been three years. I've made it easy for Owain to believe, but the playact isn't the only reason I'm still in his company.

Nest was right. He was never going to let her go.

He won't ever let me go, either.

"So I prayed to Saint Elen. She looks to me always. I asked her what I should do. Then I found this." Owain turns the underwear charm and runs his thumb over the embroidery. "She sent me a banner. I'm to ride to war. Saint Elen is going to help me take down my father."

"Kill your—but Cadwgan's the backbone of Powys! Ceredigion too! If you kill him—"

"What?" Owain snarls. "What will happen if *my lord father* isn't around to tell me what I can plunder and when I can take a shit?"

Powys will be overrun before the season turns. Gilbert fitz Richard de Clare and his thirty land-hungry Norman knights will occupy Ceredigion in a month's time. Cadwgan ap Bleddyn is the only thing keeping his kingdom together, keeping Welshmen and Normans alike wary and reluctant to step over any of the borders. Not a man of them crosses Cadwgan without weighing it well.

"No." I'm trying to breathe. "No. Saint Elen does not want you to harm your father."

"How do you know?" he asks quietly.

If I make myself the saint, she will strike me down.

If I don't, someone in this clearing will.

"It's just that . . ." I clutch at another true thing. "You'll have plenty of time to be king. This is your *father.*"

Owain's face is slowly going hard and blank once more. This is not what he wants to hear, and a playact only works when Owain ap Cadwgan wants it to. My eyes go to the blade gripped loose in his hand. He could kill me in two motions. Owain is not used to Saint Elen working against him in any way. He is not used to hearing no.

Einion penteulu steps closer. "I'll be honest, my lord. I had my doubts about your battle banner and how you came by it, but I take it all back. At least a saint will not rob you. She will not change her tune when she's held to account."

"Your father didn't kidnap us, and he certainly didn't send a man to rob you." I edge near enough to touch a fold of Owain's tunic. I need him off this idea. That a saint might guide his hand. I need him to hear *me.* "None of this is what it seems."

"Then what *is* it?" Einion asks, soft and cutting, and he is at Owain's shoulder and they are a shield wall just as they always have been. "I'm a simple fighting man, but even I know when a girl thinks to lead me by something that's definitely not my hand. Perhaps men have been whispering in *your* ear these days, hmm?"

That's got to be out of turn. But Owain does not raise a fist. He doesn't even bristle. All he does is wind a finger around his underwear charm like these shadowy doubts are commonplace. Like it's not impossible there's something to them.

"When we were in Ireland, you wanted nothing more than to retake Powys from your cousin Madog." I'm talking to Owain and only Owain. "Now you can. Now you *should.*"

"Says who?" he asks.

I open my mouth to tell him. *Your father. Cadwgan ap Bleddyn.* But all he'll hear is *shut up and go plunder something.*

"Saint Elen." It's out of my mouth before I can stop it.

Owain squints at nothing for a long moment. "She's mistaken. I will ask her myself."

"I–I don't think saints are ever mistaken, my lord."

"This time she is," he says in a too-quiet voice.

The whole clearing goes blurry as it catches up to me, what this is. What it's been becoming these last se'ennights. *I'd much rather listen to a saint.*

This is his playact now.

"The Normans are going to raid Ceredigion," Owain says into the silence. "Since I'm still in Ireland, my father will lead a warband to drive them back into Dyfed. There'll be an ambush. No survivors. Very tragic."

No. I want badly to say it. Cadwgan ap Bleddyn just wanted me gone. He could have cut my throat. Instead he opened his hand.

But it'll be chaos. No one notices girls in the shadows. No one thinks they will do anything but what they're told.

I said I could save Owain's life. Not Saint Elen. Me. Saint Elen came later, once I realized he'd make light of the saving and turn me out once the fever was a memory and the wound just one more tale to tell around a fire. I knelt at his side as his color drained around the hilt of the butcher knife beneath his arm, and when I gripped the handle to pull it free, every teeming thought in my head screamed *twist it twist it twist it.*

This time I know enough to think. This time I must take what I want with my own hands.

There's cold meat for supper. I can't get near enough the fire. I'm still trembling. Rhys puts himself next to me, but I won't reply to any of his polite attempts at conversation. My head is throbbing. My arms, where Morgan held me. Rhys's fault, all of it. He's the sole reason I'm not under a pile of squealing, happy children right now.

He runs a thumb over his forearm and doesn't move from my side.

The lads of the warband look at me differently now. There's no more reverence. No more cautious, courteous distance. They've heard two stories about me, and even though Owain is a king's son and they dare not cross him, Einion is their penteulu. He is a man they listen to.

Owain and Einion are a ways distant deciding where the sentries will be posted, where the trip lines will go. It'll be dark soon, and Owain will come over here. He'll tuck an arm around me and slide a hand up my leg and I — I can't.

"I'm not going to tell him," Rhys says quietly. "Where you meant to go. What you meant to do."

"He wouldn't believe you anyway," I murmur, and Rhys rubs his upper arms and winces.

"Just . . . why?" Rhys peers at me sidelong. "You . . . share a bed with him. Don't you care what happens to him?"

When Owain kicked in my door, Rhys was a boy dropping worms in his sister's hair and tying thread to spiders to make pets of them. To him, Owain and I must seem as good as married. He has always seen us as ordinary.

"What about me?" I say it so quiet that Rhys must not hear. But I say it.

"I mean, all right, Owain was a bit of a bastard to you in Ireland," Rhys goes on. "He owes you an apology. But if you're not with him, he can *die.*"

I pull my cloak tighter across my shoulders. Owain ap Cadwgan owes me a lot of things, but I owe him, too. Things went bad enough for me after he kicked in my door, cold everywhere *can't struggle,* and they could have gone worse, but instead I spent three years kept by a king's son when no one but him would have had it so. There was a price, but there was no screaming or dragging. It's not because we shared a bed that I care what happens to Owain ap Cadwgan, and it's sure as anything not going to keep me here a moment longer than it must.

"Up you get, pisser." Einion penteulu appears out of the shadows and holds out a fistful of tiny sticks at Rhys. "Time to draw your lot."

Owain is a step behind him and cheerfully points at one of

the sticks. "Not that one. It's the short lot. You don't want first pull, do you?"

"I don't know much about short lots, my lord," Rhys says, "and as for pulling, you'd have to ask Einion here."

There's a moment — openmouthed, staring — and then Owain cackles and claps Rhys on the back hard enough to send him staggering. "There he is. We'll make a warbander of you yet."

Einion penteulu is grinning, too, as he nudges Rhys's shoulder with his fistful of lots. Rhys chooses a stick that's long enough that he'll get a decent night's sleep, but when Owain drops to the ground at my side, Rhys clears off without a word.

It was easy to be done with Owain in the darkness of the maidens' quarters. Easy to say it to Nest, who Owain wronged all over again every day she woke up sore and scared and away from her children. Especially easy in those early hours after he turned his back on me in the courtyard at Rathmore. It was even easy to say it to Cadwgan ap Bleddyn. I meant it every time.

But now he's here. It's the middle of nowhere and he's spent too many days listening to Einion penteulu suggest time and again that he is better than fine without me. Owain might be listening to a saint on his own terms now, but there are other things he gets out of keeping me safe and near him. Sure enough, he hooks a palm over my hip and pulls me against him. He has that hungry look to him like he does when he comes back from a raid, days away from me, se'ennights. Impatient and intent. He leans his face into my hair and breathes in deep.

"Owain." I try to pull free, but his other arm slides around my waist and holds me close. "Wait. Stop."

He rumbles a slow groan and doesn't move away, but his hands go still where they are.

I could tell him it's my monthlies. I could tell him that my head hurts from when his men slammed me into a tree. I could tell him Saint Elen says to lay himself down anywhere else but with me. Now is the time to say everything I've always bitten back. Instead tears slide down my face and I swipe at them.

Owain doesn't know what to do with me when I cry. It means he must speculate.

"Oh, aye, stop," Einion penteulu says, and there's a curious edge to it. "You didn't draw your lot."

He's back from the other side of camp and Owain cuts a glare up at him, but Einion merely holds out the lots. Even a king's son must have a turn at standing watch. He jerks a stick out of Einion's fist. A short one. Owain curses aloud and snaps it in half.

"First pull, eh?" Einion penteulu almost smiles. "Bad luck."

"Sorry," Owain mutters into my hair, and then he's up and across the clearing.

When he's gone, Einion kneels and opens his hand. There are no long sticks. Only short ones. In the time it takes me to work out what it means, he's scattered the lots and risen.

Both of us watch Owain disappear into the greenwood. Einion ap Tewdwr has no intention of leaving me alone with

Owain any longer than he must. He won't just let me walk out of here, though. If I run, plan or not, he won't bring me back this time. He'll tell Owain it was wolves. Or any of the dozens of men who would smile to see him dead.

Chaos will keep Einion penteulu occupied as well.

I'm on my feet. Trying to make him look at me. "You can't think going after Cadwgan is a good idea."

Einion snorts. "First you're telling a king's son what he wants. Now you're telling the penteulu of a warband what he thinks."

"You have to put a stop to it! However you can!"

His reply is to move away toward the tree line with a cock-sure swagger, and by Christ I will find Owain *right bleeding now* and tell him that Saint Elen would have him dismiss Einion penteulu in the most public and humiliating way possible.

But Einion ap Tewdwr is capable and loyal and keeps his head when everything falls to hell. He's the man who'll give Owain good counsel long after Saint Elen and I have gone. Einion will look to Owain even if Saint Elen does not. Turning Owain against his penteulu will put him in harm's way.

Summer twilight seems to last forever, and I'm still too trembly to even try to sleep, but I'm exhausted enough to lie down. The next moment, there's a rustling of movement at my back and a light drape of cloth over me, and it's night-black and I'm lying near what's left of the fire. Someone's just lain down behind me and I flinch, hard, because I'm not as sure of these lads anymore.

"Shh, it's only me." Owain's whisper tickles my ear as he settles in and slides an arm across my belly. I shift away, but he holds tighter. "What's wrong?"

"I just . . . I'm tired. Please let me sleep."

"But I want to be close to you." He pauses. "All right?"

All right. He held out a hand from the curtained bed, and four-and-ten-year-old me was anything but all right. She was trembling too hard to move. Hands clenched, guts writhing, frozen in the shadows. He let me cry till I was done. Then he poured a mug of wine and handed it to me without a word. I didn't drink it — too bitter — but having something to hold kept me from falling apart completely. Then he started telling me about his favorite wolfhound that had a litter of pups and one of them was red, just like a dog he had as a boy. I held the mug with both hands and breathed. Then he went on about some kind of game that he and the lads played that involved a ball and brawling and mud. His voice was calm, and he made no move toward me. At some point I said all right, and by morning I was curled under his arm and I was not nearly as afraid.

The spare gown Isabel gave me is under my head. My shoulder digs into the dirt. Owain's arm over me is heavy but unmoving. I made him believe, but every last thing he's done has been his own choice. I can't let him suspect I'm counting the days again, only this time I'm waiting for him to make one more bad decision. The one that'll let me slip away forever.

Somehow I will have to go back to sleep. Somehow, with Owain lying beside me. With Nest and the little ones so close, it almost feels like I'm there already. So I pray to Saint Elen with a new prayer, one she will have to stop and listen to, one that will not glide past her ears with the rhythm of a thousand litanies.

> *Thank you for everything you've done for me.*
> *Thank you for understanding.*
> *I will steer him away from evil for as long as I'm able.*
> > *When I'm gone, he's entirely in your hands to do with*
> > *as you see fit.*

THE LADS MARCH BURNING. THEY DO IT FOR DAYS
and days. Vale after vale. They burn and smash and hamstring.

They kick in doors.

I'm falling behind the column. The lads are shapes moving
through the trees, blurry arcs of metal and glowing firebrands
and endless, relentless marching. It's not a chaos for fleeing
through. It's a chaos for living through.

This has every mark of a Norman raid. Cadwgan will hear
of it soon. He'll call up his warband. He'll march to drive the
enemy out, and he'll find—

Vale after vale. The sky turns gray and then black.

Rhys appears. He's got soot beneath his fingernails and his
hair is just starting to curl again at the ends.

"I'm all right," I mutter. "Go on with the others."

He doesn't, though. We move together as whole vales burn. He is careful not to touch me, but we are shoulder to shoulder nonetheless.

Then one morning Einion penteulu doesn't give the order for the lads to march drawn and ready. Instead he and Owain stand together in the cold chill of dawn, deep in discussion. They turn when Rhys slants through the trees at a dogtrot, out of breath, and heads straight for Owain.

This is it. Cadwgan is somewhere close, and they'll be setting up the ambush. None of them will be watching what I'm doing.

"Can't be," Owain growls. "We are *playacting* a Norman raid. Not a man of those bastards would dare the real thing."

"Not unless he thought he could get away with it," Einion penteulu replies. "You're supposedly in Ireland. Your father was negotiating from the border with England. Your cousin Madog in disarray."

"It's half-built." Rhys is panting, deep and winded. "Norman style. The keep's partway up. Walls look solid, but wood burns."

"Gerald of Windsor. It can be no other." Owain grins at the heavens and pets his underwear charm. "Thank you, Saint Elen. I'm listening. Keep pointing me true."

It's too much to hope that Nest will be with him. Not somewhere like this. But I'll get an audience. Gerald of Windsor will know who I am by now. Nest will have told him everything, and he'll know what I've done for his children. How he owes me for leaving me stranded on that pier.

He'll know what Nest promised, and how it was bought.

We move swift and silent now. Nothing burns. There's no plunder. By midday I'm belly-down, on a rise alongside Owain, looking down toward a rolling green plain. An earthwork mound rises above a fist of sharpened palisades. A tangle of rope and a web of scaffolding cling to it like cobwebs, but it looks finished enough to resist anyone trying to harm it. Men are at their labor throughout the works, carting barrows of stone and driving teams of horses dragging timbers, and somewhere down there is Gerald of Windsor, directing the digging of the ditch and the fastness of the gate and the placement of the men who will hold it for him.

Gerald of Windsor, who is still offering a bounty on Owain's head.

Raids are done quick, like the snap of a neck, and this castle looks too sturdy to be taken by a single attack. Owain will bid me wait here where it's safe. He won't be able to spare anyone to mind me. When the lads fail and scatter, I'll need to be gone. I won't get another chance like this.

"M-my lord?" Rhys's voice trembles.

"Dusk," Owain replies, "when they're at their supper."

There's a small grind of metal. I turn and stiffen. We're surrounded. Men in leather armor stand over us, pointing long spears at our necks. One has Rhys by the collar, a blade quivering at his throat.

"Stand," one of them says in French. "Slowly."

I do it. My legs somehow hold me up. Owain always says he gives no mercy to Normans and doesn't expect it from them.

Whatever happens now, Gerald of Windsor will make sure it's anything but quick.

"Saint Elen," I whisper, because saints are here to help us for reasons none of us can know, and mayhap it hasn't been Owain she's been looking to these last years. Mayhap she's been looking to me.

Owain cuts his eyes my way. Stands straighter.

The Norman asks something. Owain responds, and the fighting man coughs a harsh laugh and stabs his weapon at the castle works. As we're marched downhill at spearpoint, Owain makes a field gesture to the lads, one I don't recognize, then says loudly in Welsh, "I told you, we're pilgrims! We mean to pray at the shrine at Saint David's, and we just lost our way."

The fighting man growls something that must mean *shut up*. We're marched through the gate, and right away Owain is pulled out of line, relieved of his sword, and shoved toward a tent with a Norman banner. The rest of us are herded toward the empty stable, and both guards tell the lads to leave their weapons at the door. Inside, Einion penteulu nods the lads into a huddle, then they pull up their hoods and rub dirt on their faces like travelers.

"We're up for trespassing." Einion speaks quietly in Welsh, one eye on the door. "If we're careful, they'll believe it. Even Normans respect a pilgrimage. So look holy."

A Norman warbander appears at the tent flap. He points at me, says something, then holds the fold of canvas open.

"You're to be questioned," Rhys says to me in Welsh, and then he says something in French that makes the warbander's face soften. The Norman's next gesture is kinder, and I follow him out of the stable now that I know what I'm moving toward.

Gerald of Windsor. Who sent the warband that rid me of Llywelyn penteulu. Who left me stranded on that lonely pier. Who's about to get me clear of Owain ap Cadwgan and back with Nest and the little ones where I belong.

If I'm to be questioned, I'll convince him that Owain and the lads truly are pilgrims. Gerald is no fool. He's done well for himself in the kingdoms of Wales, and he won't risk the wrath of all his neighbors — to say nothing of the Church — by letting vengeance so consume him that he'd punish blameless pilgrims who mistakenly blundered through his dooryard. He'll see them on their way and send me to Nest.

I can see to it that all of us come out of this well.

A man in a coat of mail sits on a bench in the middle of the tent. He's got a trim, reddish beard, and he doesn't stand up when I enter. Sure enough, there's no sign of Nest. Nothing of a woman here. I knew it would be so, but a friendly face would make this easier.

I put myself before Gerald and curtsy like I would to Cadwgan, but I'm so used to having patter at the ready that I don't quite know what to say. "My lord. I'm sorry to have to approach you like this. But I'm—"

"I know who you are." Gerald's Welsh is fluent, but the Norman tilt in the words makes me cringe. "You're the girl who Owain ap Cadwgan believes brings him a saint's protection."

My mouth falls open. Nest must have told him of me, but he's never so much as seen my face. "H-how did you know?"

Gerald sits up straighter. "So that *is* Owain ap Cadwgan who's trussed up in my gatehouse, playing at bettering his soul."

This doesn't feel right. If he knew who he'd captured, Gerald of Windsor would already be torturing Owain in full view of every last man in this place and forcing us to watch. Unless this is part of the torture. Nest never said her husband had a stomach for cruelty, but where she's concerned, perhaps he's finding one.

"No." My skin is prickling. My arm hair. Cold all down my back. "I mean, yes, I'm the girl you're speaking of, but Owain and I parted company. Those pilgrims you caught pitied a woman traveling alone and promised to bring me to you. That's why they were near your castle works. They're good men. But I must tell you—"

"Hmm." Gerald squints. "I'll just keep you here, then, shall I? I'll turn Sir Pilgrim and the rest of his very well-armed fellow penitents loose. Then we'll wait."

Gerald will release Owain and the lads, and in less than a pissing while Owain will come for me with the same hellbent rage he once expected of this man. Not just because of Saint Elen, either. I may as well be barefoot and in my nightgown.

Or wearing a collar, like a good little pet.

I will get myself clear. With my own hands. "Do one better. Send me to your wife. Nest promised I'd be nurse to your children."

"You're not going anywhere." He says it simple and final, no edge of threat or menace, but he's peering at me as if trying to solve a riddle.

"Owain ap Cadwgan won't come for me," I insist. "You can't lure him here by keeping me."

"I think I can," Gerald replies mildly. "He won't do without his precious saint. Making him safe from all harm. As long as you're near."

Nest has every reason to want Owain ap Cadwgan dead. I don't begrudge her that. She would have told Gerald everything she knew, everything she observed. The playact's not a secret — that's how it does its work — but now Saint Elen is a weapon in Gerald's hands.

I'm a weapon. And there's but one way to blunt it.

"Don't bother. It's all lies." I square up and blink back tears I can't account for. "Saint Elen does not protect Owain. She never has. I made it all up for my own ends. He finally found out. Turned his back on me. Abandoned me. He wants nothing more to do with me or Saint Elen ever again now that he knows everything he believed about her is a lie."

"Everything?" Gerald raises one rusty brow.

"He can't stand knowing he's just a man. No better or worse than any other." My belly is churning. This ends here. Gerald will have no reason to keep me from Nest. "Owain will not come here, so you may as well —"

"Hsst." Gerald gestures to a Norman fighting man standing

at the tent flap, who drags Owain in by his bound wrists. "Say it again for Sir Pilgrim."

I can't breathe. I'm trying to speak. And the patter is gone completely.

Gerald of Windsor is smiling.

Owain's mouth hangs open, making words that don't come out. Hunched over like a boot to the guts. Like a knife to the back.

"My, my," Gerald drawls, "Sir Pilgrim looks remarkably upturned for the sake of a man he swears back to front he *is not*. You, dear girl, look as wretched as Judas. I wonder why that is."

Nest would fold her arms. She'd say Owain has this coming. But she did not have to drag me into it. She could have told Gerald to take his vengeance swift and clean in a raid.

But if it's not cruel and ugly, it won't be vengeance.

"So let me see if I have this clear." Gerald jabs a mocking thumb at Owain. "You're a simple pilgrim who is definitely *not* Owain ap Cadwgan, and I definitely *cannot* lure that double-dealing son of a whore to this place by keeping this girl, because somehow she just spun a tale out of nowhere that he was fool enough to believe for bleeding *years*. So I definitely *should* let the girl go at once and should definitely *not* hang every man of you from the walls."

Owain's face is going warband blank. Like it's foregone that the others will watch him die, and he is deciding now how that will look.

"Th-that's right, my lord." I can still make this right. I must save them. "They're pilgrims. Let them go. Please. You will face Owain ap Cadwgan before you know it, and you will do well to be ready for him."

Gerald snorts and gestures, and the Norman behind Owain hauls him away stumbling. Outside, someone calls for rope, lots of it.

I scrub tears from my eyes. I'm numb.

Owain will hang. He will hang at the hands of a man whose destruction he swore to preside over. Knowing Saint Elen will not save him because she has never looked to him. Knowing it was I who brought him to this moment.

Nest will hug me. She'll tell me it had to be done. That at least hanging's clean. She will sit with me all the hours I need to mourn, and if Saint Elen has any mercy, one day the echoes of this betrayal will fade.

"My lord Clare?" Another Norman standing at the tent flap gestures at me. "What of her?"

"I've heard enough. Send her out."

My mouth falls open.

"Hang her with the others?"

"Nah. I'll not hang a girl."

"C-Clare?" I swallow and swallow. "No. No, you're Gerald of Windsor."

The man on the bench smiles the smallest, faintest bit. Then he nods at the warbander, and the world is dissolving into blurry color and I am stumbling with a painful hand on my elbow and then I'm in the mud outside the tent.

Not Gerald of Windsor who Nest promised would see us all a family. Gilbert fitz Richard de Clare. Who commands thirty land-hungry knights who've all been promised a piece of Ceredigion.

Owain will hang, this province will fall, and I'm no closer to Nest than I was when I stepped in this tent.

†

I PICK MYSELF UP. I'M MUDDY AND SORE AND MORE
than a little greensick. A handful of Norman fighting men stride
among the laborers, shouting in French and cackling. One of
them gestures to the walls and pretends to jerk at the end of a
noose like a hanged man. The rest of them roar laughter.

It won't be just Owain. All the lads will die today. Einion
penteulu. Rhys, who has barely seen a fifteenth summer.

Clare turned me loose. He opened his hand. The gate is a
stone's throw from the tent. It's pulled closed, not even latched,
and the gateman is snickering and distracted. No one looks twice
at girls in the shadows.

Gilbert fitz Richard de Clare made me a weapon. I am a
fire iron, and by God Almighty and all the saints, I am coming
down.

I sidle up to one of the open smithy fires burning in the yard and snare a bucket. Then I shovel embers inside and add some pitchy-ended staves. The stable is quiet and empty. The lads have been wrestled outside toward their fate, and all the horses must be hauling logs and stones and loads. I scatter the embers into piles of hay, and they brown, blacken, then smoke in earnest.

I will make my own chaos. I will bring down this whole miserable castle works around Clare's wretched Norman ears, and I will leave Owain and the lads to come out of it however they can.

The staves have become firebrands, and I shove them into the roof rafters until everything is crackling nicely. Soon flames are licking up the stalls and smoke is snaking from the roof-thatch and pumping out the door.

This is how the lads can do it. This is how they march burning and pay no heed to cries for mercy or pity. They are no longer flesh and blood. They are weapons, and weapons are made of iron and steel.

There's a cry, a jabbering in French that's pure panic.

Men run and shout through the castle yard. There's no well yet, no water, so they work frantically to pull down buildings near the stable with long hooks. They mean to limit the damage, but sparks leap from the blaze and catch the timbers and fall into cloaks and hair. Horses smell the smoke and start grunting and screaming, fighting to break free and run.

Rhael said not to be afraid. I am not afraid. I am bloody well *angry.*

There's a clatter at the gate. Owain and the lads have freed themselves, and now they're nose to nose with the porter, who's standing before the latch-bar with a spear, but he's also outnumbered five to one, and his cries for help are lost amid cries of fire. Einion penteulu pretends to grab at the weapon while Rhys kicks out the porter's legs from behind. Morgan and Llywarch fall on the poor wretch with heels and fists while Owain shoulders open the gate.

And he is gone.

All of it is gone. The playact. Saint Elen. Burned, the lot of it, just like the castle works. My eyes sting a little, but mostly I feel light, like the smoke drifting skyward and hazing out the sun.

None of the Normans pay me a bit of mind as I slip out the gate. They are trying to save something that was never meant to stand.

I mean to put the sun at my right and walk south, but the day catches up with me and I find an old log deep in the greenwood and sink down.

Deep breaths in. I burned a half-built Norman castle unlawfully standing on Cadwgan's territory.

Long breaths out. Owain will come after me. He will not let this lie.

In. Dyfed can't be far if we're near enough to the border for Clare to risk raising a castle.

Out. I must find Gerald of Windsor before—

There's a riffle of brush so quiet I only hear it because I know to listen. I'm on my feet, and it's Rhys who emerges first, his whole face anxious. Einion penteulu is a step behind, coughing into his sleeve. They are five, and there are no more columns. They travel in a pack now, like wolves.

Owain steps toward me, but he's not carrying a blade. Perhaps he intends to kill me with his bare hands. I draw my meat knife. If I've bought my liberty with betrayal, I can't act in half measures.

"Clever, sweeting," Owain says cheerfully, and with two small motions my knife is out of my hand and in his. "Clare believed you completely. Hellfire, even I did for a moment there! I thought I was a dead man, but Saint Elen saw me through yet again."

I blink. Not sure I heard true.

He's playing with my blade, rolling it down his hand and catching it midfall, balancing it tip-down on his finger. Like a toy I might hand to Margred.

I snatch it back and grip it tight enough to sting.

Owain frowns, then reaches an arm toward my waist. I step away from him. His good cheer falters, and he asks, "What is this?"

Einion penteulu looks up sharp, then draws Rhys aside and mutters in his ear. Rhys shakes his head, but when Einion stabs a finger and makes the *perimeter* field gesture, Rhys reluctantly slips away, looking over his shoulder every third pace.

"Saint Elen brought me to a Norman enemy," Owain goes

on warily, "and she gave me victory and kept me from harm like she always has. Did she not?"

The patter rises to save me. It tells me to put away the dagger. Smile big, spin out the falsehoods, let him slide an arm around my hips and plant a noisy kiss on my cheek. Wear my spoils, put on my show, spread my legs. Be part and parcel of whatever full measure of vengeance he thinks to carry out. Follow after like a good little pet. See to it that I'm doing all the things he's decided make a place for me with him so no one pays much attention to what he's doing.

"No," I say, quiet but steady. "No, she didn't."

Einion penteulu moves to Owain's shoulder. Gestures to the other lads to step back and stand ready.

"I beg your pardon?" Owain asks in a low voice.

The patter wants to save me, but there'll be no saving myself that way. Nest will save me. The little ones, their giggles and chatter. A family will save me. One I've made myself, with my own hands. I clear my throat and repeat, "No, Saint Elen did nothing."

"You—you were lying to Clare." Owain's voice takes on an edge I've never heard. "So Saint Elen could get us clear enough to burn the castle and escape."

I grip my knife. I lift my chin. This will save me. This and nothing else. "No. I wasn't lying to Clare. I've been lying to *you*. Saint Elen. All of it. I made it up. There's never been—"

Owain moves so quick he's in front of me while I'm still speaking, and he belts me hard across the face and I go down.

He's roaring something, hollering, animal cries, fierce, wordless, hulking above me and primed for murder.

I brace for it. The first blow. The final one.

But Owain does not kill me.

Owain doesn't kill me because Einion penteulu has him in a choke hold, one forearm across his neck and the other grappling his swinging free fist behind his back, up, up, between his shoulder blades.

My face hurts. My cheek, my nose leaking—oh Christ, blood.

"Get the hell out of here!" Einion shouts at me, harsh, over Owain's bellowing.

Somehow I'm walking through the greenwood. My feet catch on blurs of stone and branch. I wipe away tears. Blood as well.

Owain is cursing me now. Words grate through his hollering, threats and oaths that would ordinarily make me shiver because they'd be directed at someone he wants to hurt badly in very full measures.

Only now that someone is me.

His noise does not fade for a long while. I don't stop moving even when it does. Einion penteulu has to let him loose sometime. Even Dyfed and strong walls and Gerald of Windsor might not be enough to keep me safe.

IT'S DAYS BEFORE MY CHEEK AND JAW STOP throbbing. I've been among the lads long enough to know that one side of my face looks like spoiled meat. Little wonder cottagers point me toward landmarks and tell me which streams to follow, and their wives offer me oatcakes and buttermilk and hearths to sleep beside. Little wonder a steely-eyed girl of twelve summers gives me a sturdy cudgel and a blessing.

There's a fort called Caeriw where they think Nest might be. At the very least it's held for Gerald of Windsor. I will stand before him for real this time. I will not take no for an answer.

But my feet are aching. My shoulders. My heart, because I promised the little ones I'd be back, and they may have forgotten me already. It's been so many months since last I saw them, and children's minds flit from pretty butterflies to honey cake to the stable cat's kittens. David may already be beyond my help, and William may see nothing but betrayal.

If the children aren't clamoring for me, Nest may decide there's no place for me in her family anymore.

The greenwood is alive with summer. Full of the rustle of wind and the flutter of birds. But there are twig-snaps that seem out of place. Crunching that sounds too much like footsteps.

Someone is following me.

Already I'm on edge. There's a better than likely chance that Owain will hunt me down and gut me, and send someone to do it. I have no doubt the lads would queue up for the privilege. Until I reach Caeriw, I can't be sure of anything.

But after a whole day of it, I get fed up. The constant looking over my shoulder. Moving away from the thrash of branches and distant swish of feet. Whoever it is can just get it the hell over with. I pick up a smooth rock the size of a cat's head, aim true, and fling it hard with my weight behind it into a stand of suspicious brush.

"Owww, God rot it!" Rhys rises from the undergrowth, clutching his shoulder. "Saints, you've got an arm, don't you?"

I breathe steady against the racing of my heart. Owain taught me to throw, like he taught me to defend myself with a knife and aim my knuckles at a windpipe. Now he's sent Rhys after me. Of course it'd be Rhys.

"Turn back," I say quietly. "Tell Owain ap Cadwgan whatever you want. But I'm going to Caeriw. Nest is waiting for me."

Rhys rubs a hand over his newly cropped hair. "I know. Only you've overshot. You should be going more southward."

"Beg pardon. What?"

"You need to turn. That direction." He points awkwardly, like he's embarrassed. "I scouted it."

"That racket in the greenwood? That was *you*? Trying to make me walk a certain way?"

He nods, and I go limp because perhaps Rhys isn't here to kill me. I might not have to beat his brains in with my cudgel.

"Now that you know," he says, "do you think I could walk with you? It'd go a lot faster."

"I can get there myself," I reply through my teeth, and I grip my weapon in case he doesn't believe me.

"All right. But, ah . . . it wouldn't be for you."

"Who's it for, then? You?" I scowl and mimic, "I'll take her where she needs to be."

Rhys has the good grace to pinken and look away.

"It's no secret where your loyalty lies," I add harshly.

"That was before. When I believed. When we all believed." Rhys toys with his cuff. "Now you need to be far away from him."

"Oh, and I'm to trust you?" I make the field gesture for *betrayed*, showy and mocking, and shake my head in disgust.

But Rhys runs a thumb down his forearm and murmurs, "Twice now. Once with irons. The other on the sea. Twice. Nothing in it for you either time."

I go quiet. There was no playact in mending his wound. Definitely none in facing down a ship's captain. "Even if Owain didn't send you to kill me, you must be angry about Saint Elen."

"We look like fools. *Owain* looks like a fool."

"Right. Right." I snort and fold my arms. "Once again, this is all about Owain."

Rhys frowns, and I look up at him, up and up. The lads have all but made a warbander of him, and expecting anything else makes *me* the fool.

"Nest is a highborn lady. She was . . . not treated well." His cheeks are pinker. "You were. You always were."

I cough a laugh. Kick a rock. I want him to be wrong, but he is not wrong.

"I thought a lot about it out here. What exactly you did. What happened to you. And I . . . I don't think I have any right to be angry." Rhys speaks to his feet. "Not when I know well what we do. The warband. What Owain does."

I trail to a stop. Sun dapples the path and puts a chestnut shine on Rhys's cropped hair. He's scanning the greenwood like he's been taught, marking threats, always alert. He is well on his way to becoming a warbander, and he will be a good one, but if the saints are merciful, something of this boy will always remain. Rhys may be penteulu one day. Owain will listen to him. Owain will hear him.

One day, when the echoes of this fade, Owain may come to understand.

"Which way to Caeriw?" I ask, and when Rhys gestures, I fall into step behind him, but he drops back so we walk at elbows.

It's been quiet for a while when Rhys says, "I liked knowing you were around. Something about having a girl nearby . . . it's nice. I'm going to miss you."

There's a sweetness in it, an innocence, that makes me think right away of Margred. How she was all the time making promises that she had no idea would cost her someday.

"He's coming, isn't he?" I ask quietly. "You may not be here to kill me, but you'll have led Owain straight here."

Rhys scoffs. "Do you really think I can't travel light enough to cover my trail?"

"Owain can't let me reach Nest. That would mean Gerald of Windsor gets the better of him. It means Gerald wins this little pissing contest of theirs, and Owain ap Cadwgan will cut my throat himself before he'll let that happen."

"He's not coming. Owain doesn't even know I'm here."

"You—left the warband?" I swivel to face him. "You just walked away?"

"For this? Yes." There's no stumble in his voice. No worry or doubt. "Einion sent me to mind the perimeter, but I heard everything. He kept saying you deserved to die, but Owain would regret it if his blade did the work. Owain was having none of it, though. He kept swearing he'd . . ." Rhys clears his throat uncomfortably. "I'll go back once you're safely arrived."

"Owain will be furious," I reply faintly. "Einion penteulu, too."

Rhys nods. He starts to speak, then shrugs.

It's midafternoon when we step out of the greenwood and onto a well-kept dirt road that winds toward a timber castle tucked into the bend of a river. There's a cheerful busyness about this place—children at play, geese in clusters, carts rumbling—and the height of that wall is reassuring. I step onto the path, but I haven't gone far when I realize Rhys isn't beside me.

He's back at the tree line. One hand up to shade his eyes, watching. Now I know for sure this is Caeriw. There's no way a man of Owain's teulu would willingly go near anything belonging to Gerald of Windsor. I retrace my steps toward Rhys and toss my cudgel as I go.

He backs away. "I won't take a penny, so don't—"

I throw my arms around Rhys and hug him fierce and sure and long, like I should have hugged Rhael instead of aiming that fire iron at the clatter in the dooryard. Then I clap him on the back warband-style and head boldly toward what I hope is a welcome.

†

THEY'RE BUTCHERS. THEY'RE THE SCUM OF ENGLAND
who've come here, to the kingdoms of Wales, because they take joy in
killing, and here they can be as brutal as they want.

Now I'm walking toward a handful of them, big Normans
in coats of mail with their two-handed broadswords, who stand
outside the soaring wooden gate between me and Nest and the
little ones.

They could be the same men who killed Llywelyn penteulu
all those months ago in the greenwood of Powys.

They'll turn me away. They'll see some tattery Welsh girl who
asks to speak with the lady of the house — the wife of the castel-
lan, the daughter of a king — and they'll laugh in my face. But
I'm not leaving till I speak to Nest. If need be, I will scream her
name outside this gate till she comes out and hugs me.

Or bids me gone.

There are four gatemen, and I approach the one who looks the sort of man who'd sneak sweets to his grandchildren. One who might forgive my haphazard French. "Ah. Good day to you. I am come to see Nest. She is here?"

The gatemen trade looks. I go cold all over. A beardless one is shoved toward the castle, and he goes at a run, dodging carts and water troughs. The grandda grins big enough to split his face and gestures for me to come inside. Into this Norman castle that could very well be held by that blackguard Gilbert fitz Richard de Clare for all that I understand what the gatemen are saying.

But Rhys brought me here. He scouted it. I follow the barrel-shaped grandda inside.

Nest stands in the doorway of what must be the hall, the young gateman at her side pointing toward me. She's holding the baby on her hip, but her free hand is pressed over her mouth. Then she's flying across the yard, getting her pink gown all muddy, and she flings one arm around me and holds on tight. She is sobbing things into my shoulder — *forgive me couldn't help it never meant to* — and I hug her back and the baby too and she might not be Rhael but she is my sister and I forgive her.

"I told the gatemen to keep watch for you," Nest says through the choke in her voice. "I knew you'd find a way to get yourself clear. Thank every saint there is."

I can't help but turn my eyes Heavenward and thank one saint in particular.

Nest pulls away, and her whole face goes hard as she puts a hand to my tender eye and cheek. "That bastard," she murmurs.

"I told him everything." I say it like an explanation. The only thing that could make Owain ap Cadwgan raise a hand to me.

But she asks, "Told him what?"

A spare handful of people know the truth. If Owain is careful or brutal, he might yet still control the story of Saint Elen, especially if he can kill Gilbert fitz Richard de Clare. Gerald of Windsor may or may not have ever believed that a saint looks to the safety of Owain ap Cadwgan, but if he learns it's not true, it won't be from me.

"Can I hold the . . . can I hold Angharad?" I ask. "And the boys, are they here too? I . . . I hope they still want to see me."

Nest drops Angharad into my arms, warm and whole and safe. "Oh, child. William asks at least twice a day when you're coming."

William wants to show me everything. The stables. The kitchens. The horse trough that's best for jumping off. He really wants me to meet his father, but Gerald of Windsor is elsewhere and won't be back till God knows when.

"He'll have nothing but a welcome for you." Nest says it firmly, like this matter is more than settled. "He owes you. We both do."

Nest shines like the sun. Her color is back, her cheeks are no longer hollow, and her smile could bring birds from the trees. There are sticky handprints on her sleeves, and her apron is full of shiny rocks and bread ends and feathers. When William runs ahead, eager to show me something new, Nest's fingers twitch as if to grab his sleeve and hold him close. Instead she pulls Angharad tight against her, or she pets David's hair as he perches on my hip.

"Alice," he murmurs, and grips my shoulder.

At last William wants to show me the nursery. It's a little alcove in the hall set off by curtains and warm from the nearby hearth. The pallets are plump and neatly made up, and there's a bench and a coffer for sitting. It's simple, but snug and comfortable. Like the steading I grew up in.

After supper, William begs to be allowed outside to play border raids with the other boys. Nest hesitates, then nods. As he goes whooping out of the nursery corner, Nest quietly tucks Angharad into the cradle she's nearly outgrown and gestures for me to put David to bed in the pallet nearest the wall.

The hall beyond the nursery curtain is cheerful and lively, but instead of slipping out and sitting at the hearth with everyone, Nest takes a seat next to me. "I like to sit here in the evenings. I hope you don't mind. I find it hard to be apart from them. Even when they're sleeping."

"Why should I mind? They're your children."

Nest looks down. "Perhaps you'd want to leave if you thought you weren't needed here."

"I thought you might have changed your mind," I whisper. "That I'd remind you of him. Of all that happened."

Nest is quiet. "William will be seven in the fall. I know he must be sent out to be fostered soon. The Normans have a different name for it, but it's the same thing. He's going to leave home. Be warband-trained by someone Gerald trusts. He won't be the first baby of mine being raised by someone I didn't choose. But William is different. He will always be. David and Angharad, too. We survived a harrowing, the four of us, and one by one my children will go into the world where I can't protect them. As soon as they go, that's all I will be able to think about, and not knowing from moment to moment whether they are alive or dead or something worse may kill me. So I'm going to need a friend. Someone who always knows what to say. Even when things are bad."

"Well." I slide closer to her so our shoulders are touching, like we'll always be together in the maidens' quarters. "As long as there's spiced wine."

She laughs aloud. "I'm glad you're here."

"There's just one thing I want."

"Saints, that you even have to ask." Nest shifts enough to glare at me jokingly. "What is it?"

"I want you to meet someone dear to me. Margred. She could very much do with a friend like you."

hISTORICAL NOTE

Wales in the early twelfth century was a vibrant and dynamic place, but not a peaceful one. Unlike its neighbor, England, Wales had no single king, but was made up of smaller kingdoms whose rulers fought constantly with one another over borders and resources. Welsh kings exercised their authority through the warband, a group of men who engaged in raiding, pillage, and targeted violence as a form of domestic and foreign policy. A warband was flexible, mobile, and self-sustaining, allowing a king to control his borders, punish his enemies, and make sure his neighbors understood their obligations.

By the end of the eleventh century, these neighbors included Normans whose families had come with King William I during the 1066 conquest of England and found themselves on the border with Wales. Over several generations, the Welsh kings and Norman lords fell into familiar patterns of raiding, reprisals, and shifting alliances. They would have been well known to one another, often related by blood or marriage, probably bilingual and possibly trilingual, and while they shared similar ambitions and outlooks, their goals were at odds. The Welsh kings sought to maintain their sovereignty, while the Normans were out to take and hold what they could at the expense of their Welsh neighbors.

One of the most influential of the Welsh kings during

this time was Cadwgan ap Bleddyn, king of Powys. He was at the forefront of efforts to halt the Norman military advance and send English kings with territorial ambitions home disappointed. However, Henry I of England was not entirely empty-handed; many of the southern parts of Wales, including the old kingdoms of Morgannwg and Deheubarth, were held by Norman lords. This foothold was never far from anyone's mind, particularly for kings like Cadwgan whose territory shared a border with it.

Welsh kings in this era were constantly maneuvering. Their complex multicultural environment required razor-edge diplomacy, military strength, and the political savvy to know which was needed when. Something unplanned and unexpected could easily upset this hard-won balance, which seems to have been the case when Cadwgan's oldest son, Owain, engaged in his most famous act.

Historians agree that the abduction of Nest probably happened, although the way in which the story made it down to the modern era has complications. It appears in only one chronicle, the *Brut y Tywysogion* ("Chronicle of the Princes"), and the account was not written at the time of the events described. One prominent scholar, Dr. Kari Maund, has suggested that this section of the manuscript was rewritten decades later, and in such a way as to glamorize the house of Powys at a time when another region, Gwynedd, was on the rise. The amount of description of this event is different from that in other chronicles, and other sections of the same chronicle, and the use of dialogue is a significant indicator that this account, while likely relating the bones of an actual event, has almost certainly been embellished.

In the *Brut y Tywysogion,* Owain learned that his kinswoman, Nest, was lodged at a nearby castle with her husband, and he thought to pay her a visit. After this visit, he and his men sneaked over the wall in the middle of the night and burned the castle, forcing Gerald of Windsor to escape by sliding down the privy shaft. According to the chronicle, Owain was infatuated with Nest and took her and her children away with him, along with another of Gerald's children from a previous relationship. This act started a war, and Nest supposedly persuaded Owain that if he cared about her, he would return the children to their father, which he did "from excess of love."

Many interpretations of Owain's abduction of Nest present this romantic gloss uncritically, and while there are various reasons for this, it's also clear from the chronicle that sexual violence occurred. Warband diplomacy had specific aims, and rape as a weapon of war has been in use since ancient times and continues into the modern day. In Owain's world, an abduction such as this one would have little to do with Nest and everything to do with her husband.

Women in the Middle Ages are often characterized as powerless, and in many ways they were, but in the chronicle's account Nest helps her husband escape, taunts Owain, and later convinces him to release the children. Despite the oblems with the evidence, it's not unreasonable to assume she had brains, courage, and grit. Living in a complex and dangerous world such as hers meant that everyone, women and men, would do well to develop these qualities. Girls like Elen who found themselves in the path of a warband could hope to live through the experience—after all, the purpose of raiding was not necessarily to produce a body count—but their chances were a lot better with a quick wit and a willingness to leverage anything at hand, whatever the cost.

At first glance, Elen's relationship with Owain might seem unusual or even scandalous, but it was not uncommon for highborn men in the kingdoms of Wales to "keep" women they were not married to. Any children born to them would be treated the same as children born in wedlock, as long as their father claimed them. Medieval people's belief in the power of saints could be deep-seated and sometimes irrational, but even today, it's very easy to believe something when you'd benefit if it were true.

Nest disappears from the story in the *Brut y Tywysogion* after Owain returns the children. Owain is the one we follow, and we follow him to war. Since Nest and Gerald had at least one more child together, it's safe to assume that she made her way back to him at some point, but the chronicle is no longer interested in her. Instead we follow Owain, Cadwgan, and their allies and enemies into a complex tangle of events—seizure of lands, burning of forts, flights into exile, blinding of rivals. Nest fades into history only to reemerge in years to come as the remote and faceless mother and grandmother of prominent figures in Wales and Ireland. Our first instinct may be to feel sorry for her, for the limits placed on women in the past, but the chronicle tells us Nest used whatever influence she had with Owain to secure her children's release. Their success and well-being had to be deeply meaningful to her.

For his part, Owain did not experience any consequences from the abduction of Nest—at least, depending on who you ask. After his father's death in 1111, Owain sought and received peace terms from the English king that confirmed his possession of Powys, but in 1116 he died in a skirmish in a contested province. One chronicle says that Flemish settlers killed him, but the *Brut y Tywysogion* gives a different story. This chronicle says it was Gerald of Windsor who encountered Owain, and that Owain "was wounded until he was slain."

In the early twelfth century, it's equally likely that what happened to Owain was one day's bad luck after a lifetime of raiding, or a revenge-fueled torture killing at the hands of a patient, longstanding enemy. One of the problems with chronicle evidence is also one of its blessings—we can see glimpses of personalities between the lines, and in those gaps are where stories like this one lie.

Acknowledgments

This book has been a long time in the making. I'd like to thank Mary Pleiss, Gina Rosati, and Caroline Starr Rose for their valuable feedback in the early years when this story was taking shape.

Katherine Longshore has been a consistent source of honesty, clarity, and enthusiasm, and without her this book would be nowhere near the same.

Special thanks go to Dr. Kari Maund, a historian who has forgotten more about medieval Wales than I will ever know. Not only was she kind enough to offer a curated list of specialized resources to help me understand and recreate Elen and Owain's world, but she also sent me a copy of a paper she wrote, which I otherwise would have struggled to access. Any errors that remain are entirely my own, or are small adjustments I hope will be forgiven for the sake of accessibility for my young readers.

My agent, Ammi-Joan Paquette, saw right from the beginning what this book meant to me, and I'm forever grateful for her grace, tact, wisdom, and hard work.

Miriam Newman, my editor, shined a flashlight on all the right places and brought out aspects of this book I didn't know to look for. Working with a fellow history nerd is always a joy.

Thanks to all the behind-the-scenes folks at Candlewick who made this book beautiful both inside and out.

Thank you to readers. Every one of you.